The Courage to Love

Caitlyn Grieve

Contents

Chapter 1

It had been no fault of her own that Maia had seen the pamphlet in Wikitoria's room the last couple of weeks. Their new flatmate had said something about needing some kind of new direction in her life and taking herself out of their post-graduate existence for a few weeks sounded more like something she needed.

Stuck between continuing her major in psychology or taking up something more community-base, she'd picked up the pamphlet and read it while Wiki was out. Three weeks out of here, totally out of her comfort zone, she threw it down...sounded like something she needed.

"Wiki your rides here!" Nat yelled up the stairs, hearing the taxi outside.

"Yeah, I saw him pull up!" Carrying her bag down the stairs, grinning at her housemates, Wiki stopped. "Well, this is it, guys!"

"I still can't believe you're doing this?"

"Yip, Getting in touch with nature. Camping in the mount ains..." She animated. "Singing cheesy campfire songs around the bonfire...." She chuckled, throwing her arm over her other flatmate Tammy's shoulder. "Aww, come on; you two will love having this place to yourselves." She looked around, suddenly noticing it was quieter than usual. "I'm assuming Maia has gone on her break already?"

"Yeah, she left this morning. Something about beating the traffic on the way up north."

"She said goodbye to you, right?"

Wikitoria met Tammy's gaze on her. "Yeah, yeah, of course! This morning." She lied, hearing the taxi driver tooting his horn.

"I better get going, guys." She gave Nat a quick hug, picking up her duffle bag.

"I'll see ya in a few weeks!"

She'd noticed Maia had been a little off the last few days. She couldn't believe her so-called friend had actually gone without saying anything. Maybe this really was a sign that she needed to get on with her life.

"Alright, last one off." The bus driver turned to look at the young woman sitting behind him. "Miss."

The light blue-coloured eyes looked up at him from under her baseball cap, her blonde ponytail tucked in the collar of her denim jacket. She grabbed her backpack and stood up.

"Thanks." She nodded, making her way down the stairs onto the loose gravel. Covering her eyes from the sun, she looked up at the two large sailing boats in the marina. Her adventure was about to begin.

The Outward-Bound van pulled up outside the marina. The van door flew open and

Wikitoria grabbed her bag and followed the others to the two big ships in the marina. Adam stepped onto the ship's deck in his Outward-Bound camp t-shirt. "Alright, can I have everyone's attention!"

The chatter stopped.

"Guys and gals, here is where your journey to self-discovery begins!"

"One, two, three," He counted the heads. "Good! So, whether it be to reassess your life or find inner meaning, our team Tia, Marco, Ruby, and I will be your leaders on this self-discovery adventure! Okay." He looked around. "Right, those that arrived with me on the van, you are now Team Tawhiti, the soul searchers. The remaining group you are now named Team Mataara, the life changers. Grab your bags, guys! Mataara head over to Marco. Tawhiti team, you are with me. All on board!"

"Make sure you pay attention to your leaders' guys! Teams give each other a wave; we are off!" Wikitoria turned and waved at the team on the adjacent ship. The young woman wearing a denim jacket and baseball cap that looked distinctly like hers caught her eye. Frowning, she stepped over the hull and leaned on the rail.

Maia looked over, seeing Wikitoria looking back at her.

"Mai, what the hell!"

Maia stepped up on the rail, adjusting her cap. "Don't be mad!"

"What are you doing?!"

"I actually wanna do this!"

"Go home!"

"Wiki, don't be..." Maia casually shrugged, seeing the boats separating. "Well, it's too late; we've already set sail!" Wikitoria's brow knitted as she put her hands on her hips. Maia was proving again and again how stubborn she was.

"This is not fair, Mai! Jump off! Just jump." She animated.

"No." Maia shrugged, seeing her getting more agitated.

"Yeah, you can!"

"But I'm not going to!" Wiki could feel the frustration coming to her vocal cords.

"Yeah, you are; you just... jump!"

A slight smile touched Maia's cheeks as she flicked her eyebrow. Man, she loved winding her up.

Wikitoria shook her head in disbelief. "Seriously, I can't believe you're doing this to me, man."

"Miss Tamati!" She looked over her shoulder, hearing Adam's deep tone. "Do you want to get off?"

"No, sir." She turned, giving Maia one final glance. "I want this. I reeaally wanna do this."

Wikitoria held fast the rope in her hand. She glimpsed over at the other ship the Mataara team was on. She could see the sandy blonde hair at the back adjacent to her. She was mad and disappointed as fuck in her so-called friend. Maia knew she had been looking forward to this break for weeks! Roughing it in nature, getting dirty and sweaty. She quietly laughed to herself. This was way out of Maia's comfort zone. "Aww, babe," She relaxed. "You have no idea what you're in for."

Maia took a sip of her water bottle. She glimpsed over at the other ship just ahead of them. She could see Wikitoria sitting at the back, her ponytail sticking out from the back of her favourite cap.

She smiled to herself. She had headed straight for Wikitoria's wardrobe when she decided to do this. Nothing appropriate was in her own attire for this type of thing. Wikitoria had already packed her bag and picked out her gear, so what remained in her vast wardrobe was fair pickings. She looked down at herself. It's funny that if she did get a little homesick, she could at least smell the cologne in her clothes.

After a good couple of hours on the ship, Adam directed them to the sandy beach ahead of them. Maia stood up, seeing the Tawhiti team stepping onto the sandy shore. She suddenly felt nervous when she saw Wiki happily grabbing her duffle bag and heading off into the bush with her teammate.

"Alright, team, we will pull up alongside and set anchor. Four at a time on the boats. Let's go!" Maia sat back down. Marco waved her over. "Maia Williams, let's go!"

Her eyes widened as she stood up at his military manor. "Yes, sir!" She looked over to where Wikitoria had disappeared. Taking a quick whiff of her jacket, she grabbed her bag and climbed into the paddle boat.

Wikitoria headed through the trees to the clearing, seeing the camp ahead. "Wow, look at this place!"

"Awesome, right!" Jake, the young guy on her team, stopped beside her. She looked around.

"Are we all staying here?"

"Yip." Adam came through the trees. "Safer in numbers." He smiled, walking ahead. Jake looked back at her.

"What does he mean safer in numbers?"

"Oh, thank god!" Maia saw the clearing ahead, shaking off another bug from her jacket. She'd walked through two spider webs before noticing she had gone off the track. She ran, catching up with the others as she spotted the buildings ahead through the trees.

"Alright, are we all here?" Adam looked at Marco beside him, checking over his team.

"Yeah, all here!"

"Awesome!" Adam looked them over. "Welcome to camp! This will be your home for the next few weeks!"

Wikitoria glimpsed over at Maia, checking she was still breathing.

"The cabins. Males are on the left, and females are on the right. Males, females' toilets and showers." He pointed to the two smaller buildings on the sides. "In the middle, we have the communal kitchen and hall, plus your host team's living quarters." He looked at them all. "The rules!"

Maia glimpsed over at Wikitoria.

"You are all here to better yourselves for one reason or another. You are not here to get sidetracked by cute boys or pretty girls!" They laughed. "After our activities, you will have some downtime to mingle and make friends. You can roam the island, but there are boundaries for your safety and the safety of others. Please a hear to them. Respect for each other is a must!" He glanced over at Tia and Ruby. "Tonight is about getting you all settled. So, girls, grab your gear and head with Tia and Ruby. Guys, follow us this way!"

They headed down to the women's cabin.

"Right." Tia, of Maori descent, turned around. "Chuck your bags up here, guys. Grab a brown paper bag, and we want you to put your cellphones, music devices, books, and jewellery in a bag, seal it and write your name clearly on the front."

Maia started removing her bracelet.

"Miss, I can't take this off." Wikitoria indicated the pounamu (greenstone) around her neck.

Tia looked at her, noticing the native girl's internal struggle to disconnect from her culture. She waved her hand down. "Kia kaha bub. Just this once, aye. Keep it safe."

Wikitoria glanced over at Maia, taking her leather necklace off.

"Nice, thank you, ladies. Head in there and select your beds. Then, we will head over to the hall. Make sure you have your running shoes on."

Maia headed on in with Jaida and Millie from her team.

"Oh well, bunk beds!"

"Cool, mine!"

"Bums above you!"

Maia put her bag on the bed next to the window at the back of the room. Wikitoria walked in. She headed towards the back of the room, watching the beds being taken up. She threw her bag down, noticing who was opposite her.

Maia looked up, seeing her looking down at her over her shoulder. She bent down to tie her running shoes.

"Maia, come on!" Millie yelled out. Maia stood shaking her jacket off. Wikitoria turned, watching her as she pulled her hoodie off. Maia could tell she was really not happy with her at all.

"You two hurry up!" Ruby yelled out.

"Hmm." Maia straightened her shoulders, pushing them back. Adjusting her cap, she turned and left. Wikitoria rolled her eyes and followed her out.

"Lights out in ten ladies!"

"Seriously?" Wikitoria's teammate Naydeen kicked her shoes off next to the door. "Damn, my legs are killing me!"

"If I wanted to go to the army, I would have." Jazz flopped down on her bed, watching Wikitoria walking past.

"Far, I'm stuffed!"

"I don't think I've run that far before. How far was it?"

"10 km."

Molly climbed up onto her bunk. "I just ran 10 km?!"

"We all did." Maia walked in ahead of Jaida. "And we're doing it again in the morning." She glimpsed down at Wikitoria, sitting on her bed. She sat down. As she untucked her shirt, she looked over the other young women chatting in the long room. They were all in their early 20s, by the looks of it. A mix, too. She didn't mind sharing a room, but this? She noticed Wikitoria doing the same thing before their eyes met.

Wikitoria reached for her bag and pulled out her sleep shirt and shorts. "I'm out, guys. I need some sleep."

"Yeah, man, let's get some sleep."

"Shut the door, Nay."

Naydeen got up carrying her nighty with her. "Night, guys."

"Night, everyone."

The lights flicked off.

"Night."

"Night."

Maia looked out the window above her at the clear night sky. She exhaled. "Night, Wik."

Wikitoria closed her eyes, trying to relax into her bed. She sighed. "Yeah, night."

Naydeen heard the boots at the door as it opened.

A loud whistle blew, and the lights came on.

"What the hell!"

"Good morning, ladies!" Ruby stood in the doorway. "Running gear on! You've got ten minutes! Up up up!"

Maia sat up, rubbing her face.

"What time is it?"

"Who knows." She looked over at Wikitoria, still asleep. She could sleep through anything. "Hey." She stood up, kicking her bed. "Get up!"

"Go back to sleep, Mai."

Maia looked up at Jazz; she pointed to Wikitoria.

Smiling, Jazz snuck over, crouching down next to the bunk. "Get up, soldier!"

Wikitoria hit her head on the bunk above her. "Alright, alright!" She watched Jazz laughing as she headed back to her bed. Looking up at Maia, annoyed, she swung her legs over.

Maia bent down, chucking Wiki's gear on the bed beside her. Wikitoria watched her heading towards the door. She quickly threw on her stuff and ran out after them.

The path had been dark, but the sun was slowly rising, and as they jogged down past the beach, the view was all worth it. Maia had gotten into pace behind one of the guys from Wikitoria's team. They stopped on the sandy morning beach, seeing Marco waiting for them. Catching her breath, Maia looked behind her for Wikitoria. She came into view jogging with Naydeen.

Marco started counting them off. "Good morning, everyone!"

"Morning!" They all answered, catching their breaths.

"Right this morning, I want you to take your shoes and socks off. Leave them here. Any extra clothing as well, then follow me."

Stripping down, they followed him through the track back into the grass along the stream to a muddy patch.

"Everyone in a circle. Right, press ups, give me twenty!" Through the moans, they did as they were told. They were getting dirtier and dirtier, more tired, and covered head to toe in mud.

Marco looked at them, staring back at him, feeling the effects of their morning boot camp. He dropped his head into the mud, smearing more of it on his face. "This mud..." He started. "This mud forms on us like a mask. In a sense, it's covering up who we are and buries us in the same paint. Yeah?"

They all agreed.

"This is your opportunity to remove that mask and let yourself be seen. Use this time here, away from family, away from friends, away from workmates, to finally find out who you are. What you can do and about fighting back against your fears." He looked around at them. "Take a moment. When you are ready, feel ready to embrace the changes in your life and be who you want to be." He pointed towards the path back to the beach. "Make your way to the pier and take that leap to wash off everything holding you back. Today, you start your new journey!"

One by one, they started getting up. Maia looked over at Wikitoria opposite her. She could see her face twitch as she held her internal conversation. She saw her nod to herself before she got to her feet. Her dark eyes found hers under all that mud. Maia looked up as her friend gave her a weird final nod. Unsure of what she saw, she watched her turn and started running toward the pier in a new, confident stride. Maia looked down at herself, covered in the drying clay. She laughed to herself. Who was she kidding? She knew why she was here. She nodded to herself. It was time to wash this mask off.

Wikitoria had just managed to get the mud out of her hair when she caught Maia running along the pier, screaming as she jumped off the end, splashing into the water.

"Wooah, was that Maia?" Greg from Maia's team asked Wikitoria not far from him.

"Yeah, that's her." She chuckled, watching her friend begin scrubbing the mud off her face. "I think she might actually need this too."

Maia walked into the communal hall, with Millie sitting at one of the tables. They had just finished coming back from orienteering. The other team had left earlier, as they were on kitchen duties.

Wikitoria was watching Maia with this new sense of confidence. She had more adventure in her than she'd given her credit for, and she was a lot fitter than she realized, too, taking her out on both runs with no problem.

Maia sat down, feeling Wikitoria's warm eyes upon her. They had known each other for a few months now, and having her as her friend and flatmate gave her a different sense of security. It was one of the things she quietly enjoyed about the feminine tomboy whose eyes flicked over her again.

"Wow!" Millie looked at the plates coming out from the kitchen.

"Who made this, bro?" She asked Clinton from Wikitoria's Tawhiti team as he placed the large pizza in front of them.

"Oh, yeah, that was Wiki." He grinned. "Nice as aye!" He flicked his eyebrows. "Enjoy." He smiled, heading back for the following plates. Maia looked down at her pizza, laughing to herself.

"Mmmhmm! Yum!" Millie pointed. "You gotta try this!"

"I will." Maia smiled, catching Wikitoria's eyes on her. "Thank you." She mouthed. Wikitoria flicked her eyebrows, giving her a little nod as the smile crossed her cheeks.

A few days in, Wikitoria noticed Maia was too competitive with her. They had been out kayaking earlier in the day after their run, and in the races, she had to be faster than her. It was starting to get agitating.

They split into two teams to take on the 10-kilometre obstacle course just after lunch. Wikitoria had managed to get a lead on Maia halfway through, but she'd just fallen off the rope swing when Maia flew past the other rope.

"Ahh, hell no!" She grabbed the rope quickly and swung again. Maia laughed to herself, realizing she'd finally gotten ahead of her. She stepped onto the stumps and hesitated momentarily, allowing Wikitoria to pass her quickly. "Keep up, Mai Mai!"

"Grr!" The race was on!

Coming up fast, they ran past Jazz and Frankie. "What is up with those two?"

"Don't know. There's some mean tension between them."

Wikitoria ran onto the balance beam, sensing Maia hot on her heels. She headed up the ropes. Maia jumped up onto the rope ladder behind her. Wikitoria slipped a little, bumping her.

"Wiki!"

"Then get off!" As Maia climbed over her, she tried to get her foot back on the rope.

"Let me pass!"

"No!" Wikitoria pulled herself up, causing Maia to lose her grip and slip down a foot.

"Damn it, Wiki!"

"Nah ah!" Wikitoria looked down at her. "I'm not letting you beat me at this!"

"It's a race Wiki. Can you hurry up!" Maia started to reach over her again.

Wikitoria stretched up higher, bumping her again with her hip. "Can you just let me have this!" She crawled over the top beam, followed by Maia's feet hitting the solid ledge. Maia followed her along the decking to the rope bridge.

"Damn it, Wik, it's a bloody race! Move it!"

As Wikitoria stopped suddenly, Maia took the chance and pushed past her. "Yo, yo, keep up, Wik!" Laughing, Maia ran across the swing bridge, turning to get smart at her behind her. Jazz was there running across. She moved out of the way, seeing Wikitoria still on the other side. As he passed, she moved out of Frankie's way and noticed Wikitoria's hesitation. "Hurry up." She waved Clinton past her, quickly heading back over the swing bridge. She stopped in front of Wiki, who seemed anxious. "Hey, hey." She lifted her chin, getting those chocolate-brown eyes to focus on her. "Hey. You can do this."

"Yeah, nah." Wikitoria backed up.

"Babe, come on." Maia grabbed her hand, backing up to the bridge. "Just put your hand here opposite mine."

"Aah!" Wiki growled but did as she was asked. She placed her hand in front of hers.

Maia was watching her. "And that one. Babe, come on, focus on me, watch me." Wikitoria's frustrated eyes met hers. "Come on. One foot in front of the other."

"I'm not a kid, Mai; you don't have to talk to me like that." Wikitoria's stubborn growl muttered into the air.

"Would you shut up? I'm helping you."

Maia ignored her and started moving backward. Wikitoria followed her lead quietly as Maia watched her hesitate again. Clearly, she needed to break into those stubborn thoughts of hers.

"I knew you didn't like that jacket I brought you last week. You won't wear it, will you?"

Wiki let out a breathe.

"Nah, Mai, I do. It's just...." Wikitoria knitted her brow at the change of subject. "Look, just because we had a moment doesn't mean I'll let you start dressing me, okay. I'm not your girlfriend."

"Oh, come on, don't be like that," Maia laughed, squeezing her fingers gently as she felt the end of the bridge under her feet. "Babe, you know you look gorgeous in it. Totally worth it."

Wikitoria heard the wood under her feet. She stepped back, looking at where she had just come from." Hey, I actually did it. We did it."

"Yeah, well, can we do it faster next time?" Maia started running around to the other side. "We've got times to beat. Let's go!"

"Wait, here they come!" Jake and Molly were standing next to Marco, who was timing.

"Go Wiki!"

"Come on, Maia!" They cheered. Wikitoria tapped her feet through the tyres. Maia was a step behind her, but Wikitoria was the first to clear them.

"Go Wiki! Go!"

Maia just couldn't match her pace. Wikitoria sprinted across the finish line, with Maia only half a second behind.

"Here." Jake handed Wikitoria a water bottle, congratulating her with a smack on the shoulder.

She leaned on her knees, catching her breath. "Thanks." She glanced across from her at Maia, taking a bottle.

"Time of thirty-three minutes thirty-two seconds." Marco tapped her shoulder. They had both come last. "By the end of camp, I want to see you achieve this course in under twenty-five minutes." He smiled over at Maia. "But we are here to support each other, and I commend you, Miss Williams, for helping someone from the other team. Round of applause, guys!"

Maia stood up, welcoming the attention. Wikitoria leaned back, stretching. "Yeah, alright." She joined in their praise of her mate. She stepped closer, seeing the smile on her friend's face. "I still bet you, though."

Maia stood up straight, seeing Wikitoria wink at her before throwing her arm over her shoulder and giving her a buddy hug.

"But I guess you're just going to have to deal with that, aren't ya."

"Oh, I think I can." She turned into her, her eyes flicking over her full lips. A little smile came from the corner of her mouth as her hand graced her stomach. "But can you?"

Wikitoria swallowed hard, feeling her face burn up. Her eyes fell on Maia's subtle lip bite before moving out from under her arm.

Wikitoria rubbed her face, turning to see if anyone noticed that. "Shit." She sighed, regretting them both being here. Maia was very easy at flirting with her, which was the last thing she needed.

Chapter 2

Maia could see Wiki standing in the doorway to the hall, laughing with Jazz.

The striking girl had only been an acquaintance through friends, and a few months ago, she'd needed a place to stay and had moved into the room across the hallway from hers. She had become that annoying little voice in her head, though. Wiki had an opinion on everything. Most of the time, she had been right, though. It was weird; Wikitoria Tamati put up with her pretty well, though. They had become friends, well, more than friends.

She caught those dark eyes smiling again, and she chuckled to herself. Yip, it was time she took this mask off and let everyone see exactly who she was. She was Wiki's; she just didn't know it yet.

Wikitoria made her way over, noticing Naydeen had left. She sat down on the stump beside Jake and Maia at the firepit. She had seen the guys flirting with her pretty flatmate. It was nothing new. When were guys not flirting with her gorgeous friend?

She caught Maia's hand reaching across Jake towards her mug of hot chocolate. She handed it over.

"Hey, guys, can I have a moment with Wiki?"

Jake turned, looking beside him at his tomboyish teammate. He shook his head, rolling his eyes at her interruption. "Yeah, sure."

Watching them go, Maia leaned on her hand, watching her dark-headed friend looking back at her. Wikitoria leaned forward, taking in the flames of the fire. "Heights, they just get me sometimes. That's all. I just froze for a minute. It was nothing." Their eyes met. Maia smiled at her, handing back her hot chocolate.

Looking around to see where everyone was, she picked herself up and sat on the stump next to her. Maia watched her leaning in, searching her eyes on her for a moment.

Maia's eye flicked over her lips as her shoulders dropped, drawing in closer. A little smile came to her lips as she bit it slightly. Wikitoria shook her head, her shoulders dropping as she moved back, the heat coming to her cheeks.

"Don't look at me like that." She said quietly.

Maia smiled softly, the corner of her lip curling. Wikitoria nervously pushed a hair back.

"Lights out in ten, guys!"

"I better take this back," She muttered, getting up and seeing Adam rounding them up. Maia chuckled, watching her head back to the kitchen.

"Any idea what we're doing tomorrow, guys?"

"Nah."

"I hope we're not doing anything physical. I'm tired of being sore already."

Wikitoria walked through them to her bed.

"Nothing wrong with being physically fit."

She glanced at Maia, pulling her duvet down.

"Never know when you might need the energy."

"Like running from a bear?" Millie laughed.

"Or your boyfriend!"

"Shut up! He's not my boyfriend!"

Naydeen stood up, heading towards the door to lock up. "Whether he is or not, remember no cute boys or pretty girls."

"Yeah, yeah."

"That's the rules, you." Wikitoria kicked Maia's bed before she jumped up on the top bunk this time mumbling to herself. Maia turned her head, smiling to herself as the lights flickered off.

"So today." Adam looked out at the young adults sitting around the campfire pit. "We are Team Tawhiti and Team Mataara today. Each group will be given a map, a compass, water, and food rash ins." Wikitoria glimpsed at Maia, sitting beside her. "Today, guys, you will follow the trail through the bush for a couple of hours until you reach your tent sites, where you will stay the night." Maia glimpsed at Wikitoria. "You will need to work as a team to get there. Once there, you must gather firewood, build your fires and prepare your meals. In the morning, you can make your way back here to base camp."

Clinton put his hand up.

"Yes?"

"Are we going to separate sites?"

"Correct. You will be at separate sites."

"Ah, man!"

"Alright, so pack yourselves some warm clothes. Marco and Tia will pick your team captains, and we will meet back here in ten minutes."

"Alright, let's go!" Tia rallied them up. The girls headed back to their cabin. Ruby followed.

"How long should it take us to get there?" Jazz asked, packing some clothes.

"Normally around five hours."

"Walking!"

"Yip."

"Oh, man!"

Tia watched them getting themselves ready. "Right ladies, your attention, please." They all stopped and looked at her. "Okay, now we have to say this, and I know you are all mature enough to understand what I am about to say." She looked at these young women. "You will be in your teams mixed with both guys and girls. We trust you to look out for each other, protect and stand up for each other."

Wikitoria was trying to put her shoe on. She leaned into Maia, trying to find her balance. Maia smiled to herself. She moved her hand back, slipping her hand down over her.

"Remember, we are strict on our rules about relationships of any romantic interests between any of you." Wikitoria moved away. "You are here for yourselves only." Tia looked at her watch. "See you outside in a few."

They watched her go.

"You are here for yourselves only." Millie imitated her.

"Yip, no camp sex for you. You gotta do it yourself."

"Shut up!"

Maia turned around, looking at Wikitoria behind her. Wikitoria pursed her lips, seeing the look in her eye. "After we pack, meet me at the toilet block; we need to talk."

"Okay." Maia smiled.

Flushing the toilet, Wikitoria headed out of the cubicle to the sinks. Maia came running in, seeing her there.

"Hi, hang on!" She closed the cubicle door, going for a quick pee.

Wikitoria sighed as she leaned back against the sink. They were running out of time. "Maia, I had hoped we'd get some time to talk today."

Maia flushed the toilet and headed over to the bench. She checked they were alone. "About what?" She smiled.

Wikitoria was kind of nervous. "You know about what."

Grinning, Maia stepped closer, reaching down for her hand. "Does this mean..." She looked over at the door, stepping closer again. "You want to..."

Wikitoria stepped back, hearing the noise outside.

"I have to go!" Molly ran into the toilet block, closely followed by Naydeen. They watched the two cubicle doors slam shut. "Oh my god, a nervous pee!"

"I can't pee on demand! I've got stage fright!"

Maia turned back to Wikitoria, who was pretending to dry her hands again. The horn went. They were out of time. "Wiki..."

"I can't do this with you now." Wikitoria walked out. Maia followed behind. "It's going to have to wait until tomorrow now." Wikitoria stopped her as the others walked past. "But you're going to have to figure out why you're really here, cause it's not for me."

"Oh, I know why I'm here." Maia chuckled. Wikitoria huffed, looking over her shoulder as she left.

Wikitoria walked back into base camp exhausted. They had walked for six hours the day before. Hadn't really slept at all and had just walked another five hours back. She was hungry and needed a shower. They could see the other team was back as they entered the clearing.

Maia heard her step into the girl's cabin, eager to put her stuff down.

Wikitoria found her at the back of the cabin, stretched out on her side on her bed. Smiling to herself, Wikitoria looked out the window for a second. Only Jada was asleep up on her bunk, snoring. Wikitoria put her bag down by her bed. She couldn't get the smile off her face. She stood next to Maia's bed, so wanting to wake her up. She looked over her length, taking in the curves of her hips and that firm bum. Checking no one was coming, crouching down, she gently reached over, brushing a strand of hair off her face.

"Hey, beautiful." She whispered, moving her hand over her warm skin. She let her fingers touch the naked skin under the hem of her shirt.

Feeling someone touching her, Maia opened her eyes, seeing Wikitoria kneeling beside her. She could feel her hand softly gliding over her lower back, her fingers sneaking under her top.

"You'll get caught." She whispered. Wikitoria's eyes met hers before taking a glimpse at the door. She wet her lip, returning with that cheeky grin.

"Now, if you're quiet." Her fingers slipped down the front under the band of her shorts.

Maia gasped as her eyes flew open.

She looked up, hearing Wikitoria putting her camping stuff down between them, her intensely dark eyes turning to look down at her for a second.

Wikitoria reached behind her for her towel, noticing Maia's flushed features, those blue eyes glowing. She picked up her toothbrush.

"You alright? You look all...." She waved her hand.

Crossing her legs, Maia rolled over, pulling her pillow over her head. Oh god, she was just having a wet dream!

"Maia, you alright?" Millie noticed her burying herself in her pillows.

"What? Oh yeah." She glimpsed up at Wikitoria, who was still beside her. Her crooked eyebrow was an appropriate response to her inappropriate thoughts.

She chuckled to herself. "Just catching my breath."

Later that evening, Maia noticed the time in the kitchen.

8 pm.

The curfew was nine.

She'd been thinking about Wikitoria since she'd seen her in the cabin earlier. Her team had been on kitchen duties while Wikitoria's team was out kayaking. She'd seen her at dinner about an hour ago with Jake and Frankie at one of the park benches.

"Hey Marco, are we finished up here?"

The handsome, toned leader turned around to observe the clean kitchen. "I would say so, guys. Go out there and enjoy what's left of your evening."

They walked out into the darkness, lit by the bomb fire and the spotlights illuminating the camp at night. Maia came down the steps, adjusting her eyes to find Wikitoria. She was sitting with a group of them around Jake and his guitar singing. She walked around the side, trying to stay in the dark, hoping to get Wikitoria's attention.

Wikitoria saw something move in the darkness ahead of her. She could just make out the blonde hair and her t-shirt. She shook her head. Honestly, she dreaded the thought of having no clothes in her wardrobe when they got home. She chuckled, though; Mai looked good in her clothes.

Maia indicated for her to follow.

"Be back soon, guys." Wikitoria got up, heading the other way until she was under darkness, heading for where Maia had been. She put her hand before her, leaning on the big Kauri tree.

"Maia?" She whispered, looking around, listening for movement. "Come on, where are you?"

"I'm right here."

She heard the whisper just before a hand touched her arm. Wikitoria turned around, keeping the tree beside her. "It's pitch black out here! There's like possums and stuff!"

"I don't want anyone to see us."

Wikitoria could feel her moving against her. Her hand slipped around to her cheek. "Look, Mai..."

Maia stepped into her, and Wikitoria pushed her back. Noticing the light on the corner of the tree, she reached down for her hand, pulling her around. Those light blue eyes suddenly bounced back at her. She relaxed. "There you are."

Maia could now see her, too. Smiling, she moved back against the tree, pulling her with her.

Wikitoria felt the tug, her body squashing Maia's against the tree.

"I've been thinking about you," Maia whispered, her fingers sliding up Wikitoria's arms to her neck, curling into her ponytail.

Wikitoria felt the fine hairs on her neck stand up. She pulled back.

"Listen, I've been thinking about you too." She moved back. "We really need to talk."

Maia bit her lip. She could see the moonlight in Wikitoria's eyes. Wikitoria watched her step into her, wrapping her fingers in her hair.

"Hey, Nah." Wikitoria reached up, removing them. "Mai, come on, you need to stop this!"

"Wiki, it's okay, no one-"

"No!" Wikitoria stepped back, pushing her away. "I don't want this!" She growled.

"Wiki, but you-"

"No, It's too late, Maia!" She bit, finally saying it out loud.

"It was a mistake! Okay, I don't want you!"

Maia returned to the shared cabin, trying to hide the redness in her eyes. Reaching for her pj's, she looked up at

Wikitoria on the top bunk facing the wall. Sighing, she leaned on the frame momentarily, wondering what she had done wrong. The lights flicked off, and she was standing there in the dark.

"Night, everyone."

"Night."

"Night."

She looked at the dark silhouette with her back to her. Wikitoria had to know she wanted to be with her for real. She just had to stop fighting it.

Wikitoria could feel her behind her. Her breathing hit her ears. Curling up tighter, she heard her move and her bed creek as she got into it. Opening her eyes, Wikitoria let the tears she'd been holding fall over her nose onto the pillow. No, she told herself. Maia was just going to have to deal with it. She'd already decided to move on from her spell on her. That's why she was here. To move on from Maia and get her the hell out of her system.

Chapter 3

Wikitoria had felt it this morning. She'd jumped down from the top bunk only to meet Maia's stern eyes. She stood up straight, trying to ignore the hurt she knew she had caused her. She wet her lips.

"Morning."

Maia finished tying her ponytail. She grabbed her cap and left without a word.

"Oh, man." Wikitoria followed.

"What's up with Maia this morning?" Naydeen jogged up beside her as they came over the bridge. Wikitoria stretched out her arms, trying to untighten her shoulders.

"I don't know. Why's that?" They rounded onto the beach.

Naydeen shrugged her shoulders. "She's running pretty heavy. Got something on her mind, I think." As they slowed down to catch up with the others, Wikitoria noticed how different Maia was holding herself today.

"Shit." She quietly said to herself, rubbing her hands over her face.

She needed to fix this.

Maia was trying to ignore her. She could feel her eyes on her, but it wasn't going to work. The anger was coming to the surface with every press-up she did into the mud. Wikitoria had hurt her, blatantly disregarding her feelings.

"Stuff her." She said to herself. She picked up a handful of mud, washing her face in it. She was starting this again. She stood up, getting ready for the pier and washing Wikitoria out of her system.

Wikitoria stood there, knowing exactly what she was doing. She was letting her go.

A couple of days later, they set off on their morning run. Wikitoria admitted she was lagging purely to watch Maia run. She was staying in step with her and noticed they were keeping quite a good pace. She had naturally assumed she was in better shape than the blonde academic. Yet Wikitoria could see she was definitely in good shape in front of her. She smiled to herself. Really, she didn't care what shape she was in; Maia was Maia.

She was so engrossed in her thoughts that she banged into her.

"Woo, Maia, what..." She stumbled over her, realizing she had stopped.

"Aah!" Maia fell to the ground.

"Shit, Mai, you alright?" Wikitoria put her hand on her shoulder. Maia moved her leg around.

"My ankle, uh." She grabbed it in pain. "I've hurt my ankle!" Wikitoria looked up to see who was around. Frankie and Lindon came around the track.

"Hey, hey guys! Can you help!"

"Who's that?" Adam pointed out.

Ruby covered her eyes from the rising sun. "One of the girls." They saw the boys carrying her around the bend to the finish line. Ruby bent down next to Maia as the boys sat her on the log. "What happened?"

Maia adjusted her cap. "I think I've rolled my ankle."

Wikitoria stopped in front of them. "She just stopped in front of me. Is she ok?" Ruby felt her lower leg.

"We'll get Tia to have a look. Guys, do you mind taking her back to camp?" Maia stood up, swinging her arms over their shoulders again. She frowned at Wikitoria; this was all her fault!

Tia came back into the women's cabin. Maia had her ankle up on the opposite bed. "Well…" Tia sat down next to her. "It's not too serious, but it has put you out of the overnight camp tonight. You cannot walk that distance, and we can't get you up there any other way." Maia sighed, looking at her wrapped ankle.

"So, I'm going to be staying here by myself?"

"No, someone will have to stay behind with you." Wikitoria noticed Frankie about to step forward.

"I will." She got in first. "Look." She sat down on the bed next to Maia's foot. "I kind of feel bad that I tripped over you. This is my fault." She looked at Maia. "Let me make it up to you." Maia looked next to her at Tia.

"If you're fine with that?" Tia asked. Maia glimpsed back at Wikitoria, trying not to frown.

"Sure. I mean, she sleeps across from me anyway, so..."

"Okay then." Tia looked at Wikitoria. "I better give you a key to get into the kitchen tonight. Can't have you starving yourselves." Wikitoria got up behind her to follow. She gave Maia a little smile. Maia put her head in her hands. If she didn't know any better, she would have thought Wikitoria planned this.

Maia looked at Wikitoria sitting beside her on the log by the fire pit, waving bye to the others as they left. Wikitoria could see her out of the corner of her eye. She started laughing. Maia punched her in the arm a couple of times.

"If I didn't know better, I would think you planned this!"

"Hey, I'm not the one who rolled her ankle."

"No, you rolled my ankle, and now, I'm stuck here with you."

Wikitoria raised her eyebrow. "Yo, I could have gone with them and let someone else babysit you. Frankie was keen to spend the night alone with you. Bet you would have liked that."

"Excuse me?"

"Lucky, I know how to handle you." She stood up, grabbing the crutch beside her patient's foot.

"You take that back!"

Wikitoria looked at her sideways, picking up the other crutch.

"Do you remember when, and I still protest, I hit you in the ankle with my hockey stick in the community game we had?"

"Yes, I remember, and you did!"

Wikitoria helped her steady herself on the crutches. "You ran me ragged, man! Wiki, can you get me my socks? Can you get me my blanket, Wiki? I'm hungry; can you make me a pizza."

"Mm, now your pizza IS amazing."

Maia reached out, pulling her closer. "The point is..." Maia smiled at her, causing Wikitoria to forget what she was saying.

She laughed. "You're point?"

Wikitoria relaxed as a smile crept onto her cheeks. "We actually have the whole camp to ourselves." She helped with her balance.

"Don't get too excited. Don't forget you are my nurse, Nurse Tamati." She let her hold her arm as she hopped forward.

Wikitoria closed the gap, looking down at her ankle. "Yeah, yeah, I know. But right now, I'm starving." She started running off, leaving her there.

"Hey!"

"Jokes!" She laughed, coming back. "Come on, I'll make us some lunch."

Wikitoria looked over her shoulder at Maia, trying to get comfortable at a table in the empty hall.

"Hey." She dried her hands. "Come here."

Maia looked up, seeing her coming her way. "Where are we going?"

"Nowhere." She helped her up. She walked her over to the bench beside where she was working. "Here, jump up."

"I can't sit up there. It's food prep!"

"Jesus! Here." She pulled off her jacket. "Now it's covered." Maia stepped back, and with a push from Wikitoria, she sat up on the bench. Wikitoria pulled over two chairs, putting them back-to-back with the rolled-up blanket Maia had used to rest her foot on. "Better?" "Maia nodded. Wikitoria went back to her pizza dough mix.

Maia leaned against the wall, watching Wikitoria make her famous family pizza. "How many times have you made this?"

Wikitoria stopped for a minute. "Man, umm maybe..., if I don't count that time, I tried to make a business out of it... maybe twenty-thirty times." She smiled.

"Is that because we always ask you for it?" Wikitoria looked up at her. Her eyes were smiling.

"Yeah. And besides, it's my go-to. Nah." She laughed. "Reminds me of Nan, Koro back home. My brother used to make us this all the time. Reminds me of home. It gets me thinking about how far I've come. I enjoy making it. Family tradition." She laughed. Maia relaxed back.

"Oh, I'm so glad we don't have to listen to Millie and Jazz snoring tonight. They are the worst."

"I know, right? I think we better take advantage of this quietness before they come back. I wonder how Nat and Tamz are doing without us?" She stopped a minute, looking at Maia. "Do they even know where you are?"

"Yeah, of course. I'm in Auckland."

"Maia! You didn't tell anyone where you were going?"

Maia shrugged. "As far as they know, I'm staying with a friend in Auckland for a few weeks." Wikitoria shook her head.

"Yeah, I knew you hadn't gone to Auckland."

Maia laughed to herself. "Where did you think I was?"

Wikitoria put her knife down. "I had hoped..." She stopped next to her. "That you hadn't bloody swindled your way into my Outward-Bound experience."

"Aww, and now look at us." Maia shrugged, still dropping her head, actually regretting the last few days. "I was hoping this would help me clear my head and decide what I'm actually doing with my life." She watched Wikitoria making their pizza. "I think I've given up on wanting to be a psychologist. I don't think my heart is in it anymore." Wikitoria looked over at her.

"Wow, I mean, you've wanted to do that for as long as I've known you. What's changed?"

Maia leaned back against the wall, enjoying this chat.

"I think I see the world differently than I used to." She glimpsed at Wikitoria. "Nat wants to go nursing. You're volunteering over at the youth centre. Really making a difference. I guess I've seen there are more rewarding ways to help people than sitting in a room saying, 'And how does that make you feel?'"

Wikitoria closed the oven door. "Hmm," She turned around, tutting her chin. "And how does that make you feel?" She joked, coming back over to her with that grin. She stopped beside her." Nah, you can still make a name for yourself. Just do it from the heart instead of trying to make money out of it. It will feel more rewarding."

Maia smiled up at her. She reached down for her hand, pulling her around between her legs. Wiktoria sighed, maneuvering around the chair.

"Maia..."

"If this is not what you want, it's fine. I mean. I'm not even sure if it's because we're away from home or because you just make me..." Wikitoria saw the lip bite.

"Woo." She looked at her a moment. "So, you're being like this here because you're horny?"

"That's not what I said."

"Well, that's what I'm hearing!" She stepped back.

"Wiki, that's not..."

"No, Maia, if you wanted a 'holiday fling', you could've picked anyone else here. Not me!" She looked over, checking her pizza. She had a few minutes. "I'm going outside."

"Wiki!" Maia called out, watching her step out the door. She sat back, putting her ankle back up on the chair. "I guess I'll stay here then."

Wikitoria looked out at the empty camping ground. This would be typical Maia. Thinking she could just use her for her own pleasure now that they had become friends with benefits. It just pissed her that she was so easy at it. She wished she could be like that.

Sighing, she turned around and walked back inside. She noticed Maia still sitting up on the bench. Crap, she'd just left her there.

"How's it looking?" Maia asked quietly, not wanting to move. Mainly cause her bum was going numb.

"It's alright." Wikitoria looked over at her, not wanting to admit she was being the stubborn one. Maia chewed her lip. She wanted to get down but wasn't going to ask for Wikitoria's help. Moving her stiff body, she pulled her half-asleep leg down onto the chair facing her. She pushed the chair to give herself enough room to get down.

Wikitoria watched her drop herself down onto the ground. Waiting for the blood to run back down to her good foot, she held onto the workbench and hopped over to where Wikitoria was standing. Wikitoria stood there with her arms crossed. Maia stopped in front of her.

"Wiki, please." She pulled at Wikitoria's arm, trying to get her to let her guard down.

Sighing, Wikitoria uncrossed her arms. Maia hopped closer, using the bench space behind Wikitoria to balance. Sighing, she looked up at her tensed-up features.

"Remember our first real day here? We were in the mud pit, and Marco said something about being our true selves and washing off our masks. You stood up and looked at me." A smile came to her features. "I realized then that it wasn't about what career I wanted to do; it was about being happy." Her eyebrow tweaked. "And you make me happy."

Maia saw her laugh to herself.

"Hard to believe I know." She rolled her eyes, smiling. "But you do." She paused. "I just wanted you to know that."

Wikitoria took a deep breath, watching her for a moment. She wet her lips. "Yeah, I um...." She rubbed her nose. "I did look over at you." Her eyebrows rose as she admitted to herself the truth. "Truth is, I was actually saying goodbye."

"What?" Maia hopped back a bit.

Wikitoria sighed. "Look, I see you every day, Mai," She noticed her moving back. "Look, I may not have come to your conclusion. Quite the opposite, in fact!" She chuckled. "But Maia, it makes sense. I decided that the only way I could focus on what I want to do with my life is to move out." Smelling the pizza, she quickly turned to check it.

"So when we get back...Maia?" She turned back around only to see her heading towards the door.

Chapter 4

I would rather have been on the overnight with everyone than be left here practically on my own with you!"

"Oh, thanks!"

The silence was starting to play on Wikitoria's nerves. She watched Maia hop her way out from the toilet block. "It's kind of creepy."

"No kidding!" Maia stopped beside her, leaning on her shoulder. "I really need to get off my feet, Wiki. It's going to get dark soon."

"Yeah, I know." She looked down at her. "It's so quiet in the cabins, though. No radio, no tv, it sucks."

Maia looked around for a minute. "Surely, they would need to know the weather and stuff. There must be a TV, radio or even a computer here. What keys have you got?" Wikitoria reached down into her pocket. She pulled out the bundle.

"A few." She looked. "Here." She handed her the crutches. "Are you alright to get over to the fire pit? I'll try these out, then come get you."

Maia watched Wikitoria head over to the storeroom, the shed, and the leaders' cabin. The door opened. Wikitoria looked back at her with her mouth open. She pushed the door open and slowly went in. It looked plain, like their cabins. Nothing exciting. She was about to turn around when she noticed a dim light coming from the back. "Well, I'll be.."

Maia saw her step out of the leaders' cabin. "Well?" She watched her walk up to her, trying to hide her grin.

"Oh, you've gotta see this." She put her arm over her shoulder. Holding the crutch in her hand, she walked her over to the cabin.

"Wik, this looks like ours."

"Just wait. Keep going to the back." She walked her around the back half of the wall.

"Oh, no way!" She hopped over to the couch, seeing the large TV on the wall. "Does it go?" She sat down, feeling the softness under her bum. Wikitoria reached behind the TV, finding the power button. Voices came to the screen. "Oh yes! Yes, Wiki, we have a tv!" Wikitoria stepped back, looking at the screen.

"Oh yes, Man, I've missed you." She directed to the moving pictures. "Ok, so." She looked around. There was a small kitchen with a jug and toaster. A fridge, microwave, and little cooktop. She looked at the TV again, and Maia sitting on the couch.

Maia watched her walk past her back to the front of the cabin.

"What are you doing?" She heard her moving something banging into the wall. She saw her come back through the door, dragging a single mattress.

"Put your legs up."

Maia swung her legs up onto the couch so Wikitoria could put the mattress down in front of it. She pulled the cushions off the chairs and threw them at Maia's feet. "Here." She passed her the remote. "I'll be back." She headed to the women's cabin and grabbed her and Maia's bedding and PJs. Maia saw her walk through the doorway, her arms full of stuff.

"Wiki, we are not moving in."

Wikitoria dropped everything on the floor. "For tonight we are." She threw their pillows on the mattress and made the bed up. Maia sat there watching her make it with expert hands. Wikitoria stopped for a moment to decide what to do next.

"Wiki." Maia's voice rang in her ears.

"Yeah?"

"Come here." As Wikitoria stepped closer, Maia turned to put her feet on the ground. She reached up and grabbed a fist full of Wikitoria's singlet. Wikitoria dropped to her knees on the mattress, laughing.

"Yes?" She grinned, being pulled closer until she stopped between her legs.

Maia laughed with her as she leaned in to kiss her.

Wikitoria's eyes quickly fell to her lips. She wet her own moving back. "Hey, come on...." A smile came to the corner of her mouth. "Stop this. We are not doing this, Especially here."

"Doing what?" Maia played, taking the opportunity to touch Wikitoria's skin.

"Like..." She knitted her brow, more frustrated with herself for being do defensive. "Like we are together or something."

"Or something." Maia leaned in.

"Mai..." She sighed.

Maia leaned forward, taking her lips in her own. Wikitoria pulled back. Maia tugged her close again, kissing her this time with more want. Fighting with herself, Wikitoria's fingers flexed before her hands accidentally touched Maia's thighs, pulling herself up between them and deepening their kiss. Maia moaned, wrapping her arms around her neck as she felt their bodies touch. She could feel Wikitoria's hands moving over her hips, pulling her closer. Her hands were about to circle up under her top. Maia flicked her tongue against Wikitoria's full lips, unable to stop what she had started. Abiding, Wikitoria opened her mouth, letting their tongues meet.

Finally, the moan came from her throat; sliding her hands around to her ribcage, feeling herself craving more, Wikitoria pushed herself back.

Maia looked at her in front of her, her eyes closed, trying to compose herself. Opening them, Wikitoria searched the now glowing eyes looking back at her. She pursed her lips, return-ing her hands to Maia's thighs. She scratched her forehead.

"Umm..." She shook her head, taking her hands off her. "What, what do you want for dinner?"

"You." Maia leaned in.

Wikitoria blushed, moving back. "Umm, no." She scratched her head. "I mean, like food-wise." She got up quickly, putting some distance between them. Maia could see how bright her eyes had gone.

"Whatever you can find."

Wikitoria stood there a moment, tasting her lips. She could still feel her warmth against her. For the first time, she could see the curves of her body through her clothes. God, she wanted that.

"Wiki?!" Maia saw her chewing her lip, her eyes somewhere on her body. She reached over for a cushion, throwing it at her.

"Hey!" Wikitoria bent down to pick it up.

"Stop undressing me with your eyes then!"

"I wasn't!" She blushed. "I was thinking about my stomach!" She threw the cushion back at her, grabbing the keys from the table. Maia watched her from the couch.

"Don't lie; you were thinking about me naked again." She reached out, tapping her ankle as she stepped over the mat-tress towards the doorway.

"Stop it!" Wikitoria smacked her hand away. "I need to get us some kai (food) and lock up." She stopped a moment, seeing the smiling eyes looking up at her. "You just stay put, okay. Rest that ankle." Maia watched her disappear out the doorway. She grinned to herself. No one had made her feel like this before. She looked up at the entrance, thinking about what had just happened. Yip, she definitely wanted more of that.

Maia glimpsed over at Wikitoria in the kitchen again. How could she go from being her flatmate to someone she couldn't keep her hands off? She heard the noise coming from the TV. She hadn't been paying much attention since Wikitoria had been standing there the last few minutes.

Wikitoria could feel her eyes on her. Every time she looked over her shoulder to check on her, Maia looked back at her.

"Can you stop it?"

"No."

"Mai, you're making me conscious of what I'm doing!" Not hearing a reply, she turned to see her injured friend getting up off the couch. "Where are you going?"

"I'm coming to help you."

"You need to rest."

"I need to move around." Maia hopped over to her. "Besides, I need to give my foot a stretch." She stopped behind Wikitoria, seeing what she was doing. "What can I help with?"

"Honestly, babe, I'm fine." She saw the grin come to Maia's cheeks. She rolled her eyes.

"You just call me babe." Maia teased.

Wikitoria blushed a little, turning back to what she was doing. She cleared her throat. " I said brah, but it sounded more like a cough, bra-be."

"Sure." Maia hobbled closer, slipping her hand down her back.

"Mai..." Wikitoria could feel her behind her. She was touching the skin on the back of her shoulders.

"Mmm." She gently pressed against Wikitoria's back, slipping her hands under her singlet.

"Maia!"

"Just ignore me." Her hands came around the front, touching her stomach. Wikitoria could feel her breath against her neck as she leaned back into her slightly.

"I thought you said you were going to help me." Her voice broke a little. She couldn't deny the little nerve under Maia's lips on her neck was travelling down to between her legs.

"I'm supervising."

"That is so not what you're doing." Wikitoria chuckled, her hold on her knife tightening.

"Okay," Maia whispered in her ear. "I'm seeing how long it takes me to break your concentration."

Wikitoria laughed to herself. "Hey, I'm not that easily distracted."

"We'll see." Maia moved her hand, slipping her fingers under the band of Wikitoria's shorts.

"Woo." Wikitoria dropped her knife quickly, stopping the hand in her pants. "Maia, far stop it!" She turned around, dropping her hand. Maia noticed the seriousness on her face.

"Sorry. Did I go too far?"

Wikitoria leaned back against the bench, trying to compose her words. She bit her lip hard. "Look, I haven't had much experience with this stuff. Okay, I'm...new to this."

"Now I know you're lying." Maia touched her tattoo with her fingers, meeting her eyes. Wikitoria's face twitched as an uncontrolled grin spread across her face.

"I'm more confident when I'm drunk."

Maia's body sighed, clearly remembering what happened a few weeks back between them. "We weren't that drunk, and you were definitely confident in what you were doing." Wikitoria leaned back against the bench. She knew exactly what she was doing when she stubbled into Maia's room after they had been flirting all night at a flat party. She paused.

"You have high expectations, Mai, way higher than me," She turned back around, picking up her knife.

Maia laughed softly, leaning into her shoulder and looking her over for a minute. "I have no expectations of you. I enjoy your surprises." Wikitoria relaxed as she gave her a little smile over her shoulder. Maia squeezed her arm. "And I'm not experienced either, so I'm not easy.

"I didn't say you were." Wikitoria tilted her head, relaxing into herself a bit more. "But, gees, your self-confidence is crazy!"

Maia smiled to herself, still standing close enough to smell her skin. "No, I can just be myself with you. I don't feel like I have to be perfect with you."

Wikitoria turned back around, a cheeky grin growing on her face. "You're definitely not perfect. Ouch!" Seeing that grin, Maia leaned in, kissing her softly. Wikitoria opened her eyes, a slight blush crossing her cheeks as her eyes fell to those lips. Her eyebrow rose. "So, you still wanna help me?"

Maia shrugged her shoulders, moving back. "I just did, didn't I?" She winked, heading back to the couch.

Wikitoria closed the door from the leaders' bathroom. She suddenly felt self-conscious, wearing only her bed shorts and a singlet. She was practically naked. She could see Maia lying on the couch, watching the movie on the TV screen. They hadn't noticed how dark it had gotten until the light from the TV lit up the room. She sat back down on the mattress, leaning back against the couch. She felt the gentle pressure of Maia's leg touch the back of her shoulders. Her pulse jumped as she handed up her hot chocolate.

"Thanks." Maia took it from her hands. She was thinking about the others coming back in the morning. This was going to be the only time they were alone. She glimpsed down at

Wikitoria's toned legs while sipping her hot chocolate. It was getting late.

Wikitoria felt the couch move as she got up, heading to the bathroom.

Returning, Maia stopped before her, wearing only her singlet and bed shorts. Wikitoria looked up at her, taking another sip of her hot chocolate.

"Okay."

Wikitoria swallowed. "Okay, what?"

Maia stepped over her. Wikitoria quickly put her drink down, getting an eye full of her naked boobs as Maia found her way onto her lap. She rolled her eyes.

"Maia, you're not helping me by...."

"Shh, yeah, I am." She got comfortable on her before she met her eyes. Dropping her shoulders, she let her fingers play with the hem of Wikitoria's shorts. "Are you serious about letting me go?" She felt Wikitoria's fingers touch her thigh gently before the tough girl tucked her hands behind her back.

"I need too. I need to find a purpose, something to do." She noticed her soft features looking back at her. "It's not you," Wikitoria whispered, touching her skin gently before tucking her hand back again. "But I'm not staying okay."

Maia searched her eyes for a moment. "Fine." She nodded. "Then I guess tomorrow we can go back to pretending we are strangers." She rose to her knees, reaching for her hot chocolate at the end of the couch. Wikitoria breathed her in as she pressed against her, her exposed skin touching hers. Biting her lip, her hands found her waist steadying her as she returned to sitting in her lap. Meeting her eyes, Maia could see Wikitoria knew precisely what she was doing. She tried to hide her smile as she sipped her cup. "I mean, it's only a couple of weeks, right?" She pursed her lips, leaning in a little, pressing into her. "We probably won't be alone like this again."

Wikitoria closed her eyes a moment; shaking her head, she laughed. "It's against the rules, Mai."

Maia shrugged.

"Oh, I don't know what you're talking about, Miss Tamati. Besides..." She whispered seductively, her lips breathing against her neck. "Nobody knows we are here; who is going to find us?"

Feeling her deliberately rocking her hips pressing into her, a slight moan escaped Wikitoria's throat as Maia teased her. "Mai," She pursed her lips hard, her hands clenching at her sides, trying not to give in.

"Hmm." Maia's eyebrow rose as she stopped. "Ok then," She reached beside her for the remote, about to break contact. "We can just watch the TV then."

As she went to move, Wikitoria suddenly took the remote and cup out of her hands. She watched her put the cup down and mute the TV, tossing the remote onto the couch. Raising her knees, she tilted her chin up, drawing her closer.

Maia brushed a hair behind her ear, and a smile came to the corner of her mouth.

"So, I take it we're not watching TV then?" "Nah."

Wikitoria started pulling her legs around her, dropping her back against the mattress. Getting comfortable, Wikitoria lay down on her, wrapping her hand around her thigh and pulling her leg over hers. She sighed, brushing her lips up her neck.

Maia gasped, feeling the goosebumps in her kiss. "Thought you didn't wanna do this?" She whispered, feeling herself melting into the touch of her hands on her skin. Wikitoria's hand slid down between them. Her hips rose. Wikitoria stopped by her ear.

"You're driving me crazy."

Chapter 5

The sound of life coming back into the camp hit her ears. Wikitoria sighed as she lay on her bunk, letting life return to normal. Well, camp normal anyway. She turned over, looking down at Maia's empty bunk. She was out walking, getting her ankle used to moving again.

Footsteps hit the doorway. "Yo yo, we're back!"

She rolled over, seeing Jazz dropping her bag on her bed. "Hey, mate." She flicked her eyebrows, acknowledging her. Jazz stopped by her bunk, looking around.

"Where's limpy?"

"Somewhere. Giving her foot a stretch. She's all good now."

"I bet." Jazz smirked.

Wikitoria's eyebrows knitted. "What's that supposed to mean?"

Jazz looked up at her. She shrugged. "I don't know, really. There's this thing between you, too. Do you know each other or something?" Wikitoria looked at her a moment. What was she supposed to say? She shrugged her shoulders.

"We went to school together."

"Oh." Jazz nodded. "Well, makes sense then. I'm going for a shower. Catch cha after."

"All goodz." Wikitoria wet her lip, watching her go. Shaking her head, she couldn't believe Jazz picked that up. That meant she probably wasn't the only one. She sighed, rolling over onto her back. They'd had sex a few times during the night, but now they really needed to stay away from each other. But was that going to be easier than said?

Maia could see her sitting over on the steps to the kitchen, playing around on the guitar while chatting with Naydeen. Wikitoria had more of an athletic physique and could dress feminine if she needed to, but she was more comfortable like this in her shorts or trackies.

"So, what did you guys get up to while we were away?" Millie asked, noticing the far-away look. Maia sat back, stretching her legs and pulling her toes back up.

"Nothing much. There wasn't much to do except eat and throw dust at the wind." She shrugged. "I wasn't that much fun."

Millie nodded, catching the little glance over from Wikitoria. "You two get up to anything?"

Maia turned her head.

"What do you mean?" Millie gave her a look. She shrugged. "Well, Wiki is..." She paused, checking Maia's reaction. "She's a lesbian, right?"

Maia leaned forward, scratching her knee. She glimpsed over at the more masculine girl.

"I didn't ask, actually." She sat back a moment, noticing Millie watching her flatmate. "Are you?" She asked, trying to find where this was coming from. A slight twinkle came to Millie's eyes as she smiled back at Wikitoria watching them.

"I wouldn't say no to being alone with her for a night." She laughed to herself. "She could nurse me any way she liked, that's for sure." She flicked her eyebrows, getting up and seeing Marco was calling them. Maia stayed there a moment. Did Wiki say something? They hadn't talked about what they would say when the others returned. If Millie was thinking what she was thinking, then maybe she wasn't the only one.

"Hey,"

"Hey." Maia found her washing the mud out of her shoes; she leaned over the tub with her clothes in her hand. Wikitoria noticed her looking around. "What's up?"

Maia sighed, looking down at her. She started hand washing her stuff. "You haven't said anything, have you?"

Wikitoria stopped for a moment. A little smile came to her lips. "Not a topic I'm just so casually going to talk about, Mai."

"I know." Maia watched her get up, placing her shoes up in the sun. Wikitoria continued her washing. "Still, I can't shake the feeling that some wonder if we did." Her eyes met Maia's.

"I think so, too." Wikitoria leaned over the sink, exhaling. It would be no big deal if they were at home, but here?

"Kia Ora, Wiki." Wikitoria looked over her shoulder, seeing Tia approaching.

"Kia Ora, Whaia." She spun around, grabbing the keys Tia had given her the day before.

"Did you guys survive your night, alright?"

"Ah yeah," Wikitoria handed them over. "Couldn't do much but...." She took a glimpse at Maia beside her. "Maia's ankle seems to have settled down."

Maia caught her eyes on her. "Yeah, I can put some pressure on it, but maybe I'll wait till tomorrow to go for a run." Tia nodded, her eyes falling on the tall Maori girl in front of her again.

"Wiki, if I may ask, what brings you here to Outward Bound?"

Wikitoria's mouth opened. "Umm." Her eyes diverted, conscious Maia was behind her. She then sighed. "Well, I feel like I have a piece of me missing, and I need to find it to move on with my life." Tia noticed Maia's head tilt as she ears dropped. She brought her attention back onto the young woman who seemed confident and sure of herself but wasn't. Tia tilted her head.

"Kei hea to Mana?" Wikitoria paused, hearing her native language. "kare koe e Maia?"

Maia looked up; hearing her name, Wikitoria wet her lip and nodded.

"Ie, he aha ahau I konei. (That's why I'm here)."

"Hmm." Tia picked up the slight acknowledgment to the girl behind her. She smiled. She'd been a leader at this camp long enough to almost identify what guidance these 'students' were looking for. Wikitoria lacked some confidence in herself.

"Tomorrow," Tia continued. "Is a chance to find that Mauri, that lifeforce, to get in touch with your wairua, your spirit, and find mana, power in yourself. Kia Kaha babe, that's why we are here."

Wikitoria watched her walk off, hearing Maia beside her. She turned to finish up her washing. Maia looked up at her.

"She said my name."

"Hmm." Wikitoria laughed to herself. "Confidence. Maia in Maori is confidence."

"Haa." Maia bounced on her toes a little, absorbing this new information. Pausing a moment, she turned, meeting Wikitoria's eyes on her. She leaned in. "I just got it."

"What?"

"You do need me."

"No, I need more Maia... nah no..."

The grin spread across Maia's cheeks as she hung up her washing.

"Confidence, Maia, no...." Wikitoria shook her hands in front of her. "I need more confidence, to be brave, not more..."

"Of me. Oh, you definitely need more of me.... told you." Maia's eyebrow rose, her smile getting more prominent, enjoying this moment as Wikitoria bit her lip, standing there with her hands on her hips. She shook her head as Maia stepped closer, quietly satisfied with herself, leaning into her. "And yet, after last night, you still wanna let me go."

Wikitoria could see her writing away in her journal. She looked around the rest of the group, all confessing their insecurities in the writing exercise of the morning. Taking a breath, she waved her pencil over her blank page again.

She'd made a nice doodle the day before. She didn't get up and read out her 'feelings' yesterday either, and she wouldn't be doing the same again today.

The tapping of her pencil made Maia look up at her. She quickly diverted her eyes back to her page, making herself look deep in words.

The pencil quickly wrote, 'I am proud to...' she paused. Be gay? Her pencil ghost wrote the word.-Lessbiann?-She ghost wrote again. 'Dirty dyke', Hearing the phrase in her head, a memory of seeing her Aunty go off at her cousin for being in love with a girl.

Her eyes fell on Maia again. Nobody knew about her sexuality except for her flatmate, and that was only because of their night together. Well, two nights now. She put her pencil down; she couldn't admit this. It wasn't that easy.

"All right, anyone willing to share?" She felt Ruby's laser beam glare scan over her, waiting for the slightest movement. "Jazz."

She relaxed, putting her journal down; she had got herself another day.

Maia watched Wikitoria looking up at the Rockwall; her caramel skin was darkening in the exposed sun.

It had been just over a week, and she had yet to see her tanning friend attempt the climb.

"So..." Naydeen ribbed, nudging her in the shoulder. "You ready to shake off this...worried look you have?"

Wikitoria's brow knitted as she took a sideways glance at her teammate. Naydeen rolled her eyes.

"Oh, come on, you're scared of something, not just the heights thing." She looked up at the top of the rockface. Wikitoria followed her glance.

"By looking at you, I would think you would be all over this...." She waved her hand. "Adrenaline rush thing."

"I am..." She shrugged, scratching her arm. "I'm just not confident that...."

"She won't do it." Maia walked past, commenting over her shoulder. Wikitoria turned her head. Naydeen saw her knit her brow. "She gets to you, doesn't she?"

"No! She just thinks she's winding me up." The cheers went up as Clinton stood on top, completing his climb. Adam stepped back, handing her the harness. "You ready?" Her eyes widened. Suddenly, Maia was in front of her, clipping her harness onto the line.

"Wiki has a fear of heights." Her eyes glistened as she tightened her harness, taking the rope. "She just won't face her fears. Like me." Maia met her eyes. "Won't even chase it." She muttered under her breath, challenging her eyes.

Wikitoria wet her lips, conscious of her teammate watching them.

Naydeen smiled as they watched the blonde take to the wall.

"Hmm." Wikitoria heard her in her ear.

"She likes you."

"What are you on about?" Wikitoria slipped her feet through the harness.

"She so does."

Wikitoria tightened her harness, taking the rope handed to her. "Whatever, Maia's obviously straight." Her hands tightened around the rope as she looked up at her flatmate, climbing the wall and pulling herself higher.

"And you are?"

She heard over her shoulder. "What?"

Naydeen tilted her head, her eyebrows questioned. "Straight?"

Wikitoria's brow knitted. "Of course I am!" She clipped onto the line, stretching her hands. "I go out with guys. I've had boyfriends! Psshh." She turned to look up at the short shorts on the cute butt above her.

"I know how to chase." She reached her hand up, interlocking her fingers in the grip. She focused on Maia, blowing out a breath. "I just have to not look down."

Maia heard the clink of a harness clip beside her. She stopped a moment, looking down to her right. Wikitoria was just behind her, pulling herself up and reaching for the grip below her foot. Meeting her eyes, Wikitoria grinned up at her. Maia adjusted her foot.

"What took you so long." She teased, putting her hand out, balancing her as she came up beside her.

Wikitoria exhaled, adjusting her foot. She leaned in. "I had a great view up your shorts." She quickly reached up, ready to give her a race. Maia saw her features drastically change as Wikitoria accidentally looked down, realizing how far up she was.

"Oh god."

"Hey." She touched her side as Wikitoria pressed herself against the rock.

"I'm here. Just concentrate on me."

"I am, and then I saw...oh god." She felt her legs begin to shake. "I'm shaking."

Maia quickly looked around for a closer grip, and their bodies bumped.

"Hey!" Wikitoria freaked, giving her a nudge back. Maia's foot suddenly slipped, and her hand lost its grip. She screamed as she swung out. Wikitoria quickly reached out for the band of her shorts, swinging her back against her. Maia wrapped her arm around her shoulder, catching her breath as Wikitoria adjusted her feet, holding her against her.

"You alright?" She breathed as Maia opened her eyes, her legs wrapped around hers.

"You guys alright up there?!"

Maia looked down at Adam, giving him the thumbs up.

"Are you?" She heard Wikitoria ask again against her. She chuckled.

"I just wanted an excuse to be this close to you again."

"I'm sure." Wikitoria laughed, holding her shirt as Maia reached out, placing herself back against the wall. Wikitoria took a moment, shaking out her arm. Their eyes met a moment before Maia nodded.

"You ready?" She locked herself in, giving Wikitoria a challenging look.

Wikitoria's lip curled. "You're on."

Wikitoria was standing under the shower head, lost in her thoughts about what she had achieved during the day. The two of them had stood at the top of the climb, holding hands raised in their success. It had been a special moment.

Maia walked into the women's showers, noticing all the cubicles closed. Rolling her eyes, she was about to go until she heard Jazz ask Wikitoria a question.

"Wiki, you made that climb look so easy."

"Aww, thanks, man!" Wikitoria smiled, soaping up her body sponge. "Yeah, heights get to me, man, but..." She nodded happily to herself. "with Maia's help, I conquered that." She turned around, hearing her door latch; Maia standing there, taking her towel off. "Mai!" She whispered quickly, covering her chest, forgetting below. Seeing Maia's eyes move down, Wikitoria stepped backward, covering herself with her sponge. Her eyebrows rose as the naked woman stepped under her shower head.

Biting her lip hard, she let Maia take the sponge out of her hand and start washing. She could hear the others talking, but her eyes trailed over the curves within touch. Maia turned around, exposing herself and letting the water wash the soap off. Wikitoria stepped closer, wanting to touch her, only to meet a soapy sponge on her chest. She wined a moment before Maia stepped closer, kissing her on the cheek. As she reached for her towel, Wikitoria reached out to touch her again, only to get her hand slapped.

"No," Maia whispered. "You made it clear that you don't want me."

"Maia..." Wikitoria groaned, stepping closer.

"No." She wrapped her towel around herself, picking up her stuff. "You made it clear, Wiki."

Seeing her words in her eyes, Wikitoria let her close the door between them. Wining, she stepped back under the shower head, pissed off with herself. How could she be so stupid! She closed her eyes, feeling the sponge in her hand. She pressed it to her chest, sensing Maia's touch still on it as it grazed her nipple. She bit her lip, thinking of her naked body still in there with her. This sponge trailed over her chest and stomach to the place below. Wikitoria gasped, suddenly conscious of the others in the room. "Shit."

She turned around, leaning against the wall. Her sensitive nerves were alive.

"Damn you, Maia." She moaned, waiting for them to leave.

She walked quickly back into the shared girl's room, conscious of what she had just done.

"You took your sweet time." Jazz commented as she walked past her.

"I was enjoying myself." Her eyes met Maia's as she hung her towel over the bunk rail. A little smile hit the corner of Maia's mouth as she noticed the glowing look in her eyes. Wikitoria watched her for a moment, knowing what the time was. The room flicked into darkness, and she heard the unappreciated moans.

Maia was just about to pull her cover back when she felt a hand curl around her waist. Wikitoria pressed into her, pulling her close. She whispered in her ear.

"That was totally inappropriate and totally a turn-on." She felt Maia laugh against her. "I have never touched myself like that before." Her lips moved up her neck. "I know what I said, but you drive me crazy!"

Maia quickly turned around, conscious of the moonlight shaping them in the darkness and her being heard. She bit her lip, feeling her still against her.

"You do things to me I can't explain."

"Shh, Wiki." She pushed her back against her bunk. "Go to bed."

"I will." She whispered. Seeing her fairer skin start to glow in the moonlight, she leaned in, kissing her on the lips. Checking no one noticed, Maia stepped back as Wikitoria jumped up on her bunk. "Night, beautiful." She whispered.

Maia sighed, still standing there in the middle of the aisle. She could taste her lips, getting a flashback of them naked together in the shower, alone in the leader's cabin. She turned around and quickly climbed into her bed. Wikitoria's words had hurt, but she knew there was something between them that Wiki couldn't ignore. She sighed, relaxing back into her mattress, her eyes falling on the body on the top bunk.

"Hmm." She laughed to herself, thinking about her reaction in the shower. She rolled over. If Wiki thought she was remotely straight, she definitely wasn't.

Chapter 6

It was routine now. Lights Siren Running shoes. They had even gotten used to sleeping in their running gear. They found they were keeping pace with each other without intentionally running together. Even on this three-hour hike up through the bush to the overnight camp, they had been not far from each other. Maia had noticed Millie making more effort to get Wikitoria's attention. She frowned.

Ever since the girl had asked her about Wikitoria's sexuality, she'd just had this feeling that her Mataara teammate was the kind to break the rules and be happy to test the waters with her girlfriend. Girlfriend? She stopped catching the view of the mountains at the side of the campsite. "Wow." "Isn't it crazy..." She heard Frankie drop his backpack on the ground. He smiled at her. "We must do this bloody stuff to see how good our country is. Trees, forests, wildlife." He breathed in, letting his lungs take it all in. "but it's so worth it." He looked back at her.

"Yes, it is." Marco stopped beside them, dropping his backpack. He looked out, taking in the same mountain air. "I never tire of it." Ruby stood up on the large rock, drawing attention from them all. "Welcome to Mahau Point. You are standing in the heart of the Picton Ranges. First, we will set up the tents and the camp and then start on dinner." Wikitoria watched those carrying tent supplies head over to Andy as she and Naydeen headed over to set up kitchen supplies with several others. Once the tents were up, they all helped set up their beds. Dropping her sleeping bag, Wikitoria looked up to see Millie dropping her sleeping bag next to hers.

"Oh." She looked over the girl's shoulder. "there's enough room for all of us." "Yeah, I know." Millie waved to her spot. "I get cold at night. Figured you'd keep me warm." Wikitoria felt her mouth suddenly dry up. A nervous smile immediately came to her face. She opened her mouth, but nothing came out. "Haa!" She blushed, clearing her throat. "I ah, actually get pretty hot, sweaty it is yuck, I can't sleep next to...." Her eye caught Maia coming in with her bedding. "Um..." Maia looked up, catching her eyes on her.

She noticed the silly smile on her flushed face; Millie was standing close enough to breathe on her, her sleeping bag thrown down in the spot next to hers. Wikitoria saw her brow knit as her flatmate chucked down her sleeping bag over the other side, heading back out of the tent. "Hey, um..." Wikitoria quickly picked up her sleeping bag. "I'm just...." She threw her bag down next to Maia's, heading out into the open, finding her taking in the view. "Wiki! Help me with this." Maia turned around, watching her go with Ruby.

She uncrossed her arms, returning to the mountain view just as Frankie walked between them. "I hope it doesn't get cold tonight. Don't exactly want one of the guys spooning me." He laughed, trying to lighten the hard look on her normally soft features. He wet his lip. "Or we could just sleep out under the stars; what do you think?" Maia looked up at him. His eyebrow flicked as he flirted. She gave him a little smile before heading back over to the girls' tent.It wasn't long before the sun started to set, and not long after, one by one, they started dropping off to their tents, feeling the temperature drop.

Wikitoria walked in, noticing Maia slipping out of her top, leaving only her singlet. "Watch out; it could get cold tonight." Maia turned around, seeing her bending down next to her for her bag. "I thought you were camping out with your girlfriend over there." She indicated where she'd last seen her with Millie. "Ha." Wikitoria looked back at her. "I wouldn't be that quick to jump into someone else's bed, Mai," she pulled off her jersey, reaching down for her bed shorts. "How would I know." Maia shrugged, sitting down and pulling her socks off.

"You may be able to, but I can't..." "What's that supposed to mean?" She looked up, noticing Millie standing behind them. Wikitoria quickly looked at Maia, her eyes widening, realizing what the girl was doing. Maia stood up, watching Millie make up her bed next to Wikitorias. Her brow knitted. Knowing it would be lights out any moment, she grabbed Wikitoria's singlet, swung her around, pushing her down onto her bed.

"What are you doing?" Wikitoria whispered, slightly confused. She felt Maia tugging open her sleeping bag. "You get hot, right, so you should sleep on the end, away from the heat." "Away from Millie, you mean." Maia heard her slight chuckle. She reached out, whacking whatever part of her she found. "Jealous?" "No, I'm not." She slid herself into Wikitoria's sleeping bag. "I just want to sleep." "Sure." Wikitoria felt around for Maia's sleeping bag, finding the zip and pulling it down.

Maia heard it go all the way. She leaned up, trying to figure out what she was doing. She reached out, feeling Wikitoria's naked leg next to her. "Are you not even in there?" "No," Wikitoria stretched out. "It's too warm." "Hmm." Feeling her hand still there, Wikitoria rolled over to face her. Maia sighed, conscious of how close she was. She also knew Millie was just the other side of her. She felt Wikitoria slide her hand over the top of her sleeping bag. "You could unzip this and curl up with me. I'll keep you warm." Maia felt her fingers intertwine with hers down between them.

She turned her head, feeling her right there. She wet her lips, moving her head closer. "We are in a tent with five other women." "We can be quiet." "Wiki!" She rolled over closer to her. Wikitoria laughed silently to herself. Feeling Maia just there, she reached up, touching her face. Maia wet her lips again. She could feel her breath on her, her thumb brushed over her lips. "Go to sleep." "Okay." Wiki moved into her getting comfortable. "Night, babe." Maia sighed, feeling her wrapped around her sleeping bag. "Night." During the night, the temperature changed, and Maia woke up sweating.

Trying to kick out her feet, she found the sleeping bag's zip and pushed it down. Stretching her foot out, she found Wikitorias beside her. Sitting up a moment, she listened to the quiet and slight snoring of the girls in the tent with them. She looked down at Wikitoria beside her, knowing she was stretched out on her back. She felt around for her open sleeping bag, pulling the end over herself and moving closer to her. Wikitoria wined a moment until she woke to realise what was going on. "That better be you, Mai." She felt the body wrapping around her.

Her breath was on her shoulder. Feeling her warmth against her, Maia leaned up, grazing her lips against her ear. "I couldn't resist." "Hmm." Wikitoria smiled to herself, wrapping her arms around her, feeling her leg and hip draping over hers. Their bodies quickly become conscious of each other. Hearing Wikitoria's quiet snore again, Maia bit her lip, unable to deny her body was beginning to feel alive with being so close to her again. She flexed her fingers that were sitting on her chest, taking the courage to move her hand down. Wikitoria pursed her lips. She was in a light sleep, conscious that Maia was wrapped in her arms. She felt the fingers trailing down her stomach.

Feeling them below her tummy button, she turned her head, meeting the mouth not far from her ear. A silent gasp escaped her throat as those fingers slid over the nerves under her shorts. She bit her lip, tilting her hips up to meet them again. Maia felt her response. Wikitoria quickly reached down, putting her hand on hers. She bit her lip. Maia could hear her breathing heavy. "You want me to stop?" She whispered into her lips. "No," Wikitoria whispered, a slight smile coming to her lips as she grabbed Maia's hand, slipping it into her shorts and sliding her fingers over her clit into her wetness. She licked her mouth. "I want this."

The pink-orange sky was just starting to glow over the mountains ahead of them as Wikitoria returned, handing her hot water. Sitting down, she pulled the sleeping bag back over her shoulders. "Are you warm?" Wikitoria asked, circling her legs with her arm rubbing the back of her thighs. "mmhmm," Maia took a sip, holding it in both hands. They had been awake for about an hour, deciding to see if they could catch the sunrise. Everyone else was still asleep. They looked at each other a moment before a smile and laugh crossed their faces.

"Who would have thought." Wikitoria teased, taking a sip of her water. "Took you long enough." "Hey!" Maia nudged her. "Took you long enough." "Yeah." Wikitoria agreed, looking out ahead of them at the waking sky. "I've been hiding from my self..." She sighed. "In like forever." Maia turned into her. "Why don't you just come out? It's not going to change anything." Wikitoria looked away a moment. "My cousin Aroha, we were close; we grew up together." Her eyes met Maia's. "I kinda always knew she was...you know." She shrugged. "Anyway, she met this girl when we were about 15. She was so in love." She laughed.

 "I've never seen her happier." She wet her lip a moment. "Well, this girl's parents didn't like the fact that Aroha was Maori, and to top it off, when Aroha brought her home to meet my aunty, well, I'd never seen my cousin get such a hiding before." Maia tilted her head. "Because she was white?" Wikitoria exhaled. "Hmm, white and a girl." "Ooh." Maia sat back. She felt Wikitoria exhale. "My Aunty raised me just as much as Mum did. New times but still a little old school." She bowed her head. "I'm just not ready for their disappointment." Maia sighed. She knew Wikitoria wasn't out 'loud and proud' of herself yet, but she didn't realise the trauma she was carrying.

 She felt her hand on her leg. Linking their fingers, she had to ask. "Your cousin, are they still together, or is she still..." Wikitoria sipped her cooling water. "Nah, they broke up not long after. Sad cause, like I said, she was happy. She left to go to Uni in Wellington. I haven't heard from her since." "You think she's still 'living her best life?'" They laughed.

Wikitoria smiled, wiping her eye. "Living like a slut I bet." She relaxed, feeling a weight on her shoulders. She looked out the glowing bulb, watching the sky's colours become brighter. Feeling Maia's hand in hers and their time and place, she smiled to herself.

This couldn't be more perfect. - You make me so happy, Maia; I could honestly fall in love with you. – She saw the words in her head. She chewed her bottom lip, those words so close to coming out. Maia turned to look at her at that moment. She could see the look in her eye. A smile touched the corner of her mouth as she leaned in. "I so want to kiss you right now." Wikitoria exhaled, wetting her lips. She leaned in. "Me too." But she closed her eyes as she heard a tent zip. "Damn." She moved back, sighing.

"Well, they're awake." She sipped her water. Maia whispered, seeing Adam stepping out. "Oh well, at least we had some time alone." Wikitoria smiled. "Yeah, we did." "Morning." "Morning." They said in unison as Adam walked past. "You two ready for a run?" They looked at each other before getting up. "Yes, sir."

Wikitoria grabbed ahold of the branch, stopping to catch her breath. She thought climbing up was tough; this tramping and abseiling down was worse. "I can't." She breathed, seeing the cliff they had to abseil down. "I'll go back down the other way." "That's like an extra hour that way. You might as well stay another night." Tia shrugged as she walked past. She'd heard this plenty of times.

Jake stopped beside her, leaning over the edge and seeing how far it was. "Woo." He looked back at her. Her eyes widened. "Oh great! Well, I better get going then; gotta camp out tonight!" "Oh, come on!" Millie stopped before her, giving her a comforting brush down the arm. Wikitoria watched her hand touch hers. Her eyes met Maia's as she walked past, taking a look over the edge. "Woo." She turned slightly, seeing the realization on Wikitoria's face. "You can do it." She nodded, looking down, seeing the guys down the bottom securing the lines. "You had no problem climbing up. This is just in reverse." She gave her a shrug, dropping her bag next in line. She gave Millie a little nod.

"Millz will hold your hand." She smirked. "Bitch." Wikitoria mouthed, shaking her head. Sighing, she decided to sit down. She might as well watch. At least she could pick up some pointers or something. Adam threw Maia's bag down. "You all good to go?" "Yip." She slipped on the harness. As Adam tightened it up and did his safety check, Maia turned to Wikitoria, watching from the safety of the tree. "Hey," Wikitoria looked up at her. "I'll see you at the bottom." Wikitoria watched her plant her feet, tightening up the rope. She leaned back over the edge.

"Mai," It slipped out, Wikitoria's pulse racing a second as she felt her leaning back, the fear of falling hitting her gut.

Maia grounded herself, taking a deep breath before she let her eyes flick over to the physically stronger girl watching her. She adjusted her hand. Wikitoria's eyes met hers, seeing her lock in her wrist comfortably holding her weight. She nodded. "You got this." Nodding, Maia started moving down over the side.

Wikitoria moved closer to the edge, watching her girlfriend walking down the side. She sat back. Girlfriend? Taking a sip of her water, Maia returned to the cliff's foot, watching Wikitoria harnessing up. Millie was making it obvious she was holding Wikitoria's shirt, helping her feel safe. Naydeen stepped up beside her. She tutted. "Now, what is that girl doing?" Maia's eye flicked over her before watching them again. "I guess giving her support. I don't know, but she's annoying."

Her brow knitted. Naydeen noticed, laughing to herself. "Yeah, I knew it." Maia flicked her a look. "What?" They watched Wikitoria start leaning herself out with instructions from Adam. "You like her." Maia's features dropped. Knitting her brow, she looked up at the abseiling again. "Wiki and I have become friends; of course, I like her." "Haa," Naydeen rocked on her feet a second. She indicated to Millie up there, trying to guide Wiki on her way down. "Yeah, Nah, I like her too, but so does Millie, as we can tell." They watched Wikitoria getting more confident, making a little jump down.

Naydeen leaned into her. "I'm pretty sure she likes you too." Maia sighed, dropping her gaze to Wikitoria's teammate beside her. She moved back. "Look, I don't know what you're digging for, but Wikitoria is straight. I know she is, so can you back off." Reaching the ground, Wikitoria breathed a sigh of relief. She turned to meet Maia's eyes, except she was gone. Getting handed water, she looked around as Marco took off her harness. "Hey!" She called out to Tia, adding her pack to the waiting boat.

She wiped her mouth. "Where are the others?" She came up to the bank, grabbing the last few things. "The boat was full, so they've left for the drop-offs." "Drop-offs?" She looked up at Millie, the last to come down from the top. "We're getting dropped off?" "Ah ha." Tia smiled at her. Wikitoria didn't like the look that came her way. "Come on, grab a seat." Tia waved her over. "Check your supplies cause you're in for a long few days." The boat rocked over to the bank. Ruby reached out and grabbed the pole marker, pulling the boat into shore. "Ok." She turned around, seeing the last few terrified faces.

"Maia Williams." Maia pursed her lips, taking a jagged breath in. "Home sweet home darling, come on, grab your stuff." "Oh god." She said to herself, getting up and balancing her way up to the head of the boat. "Now remember." Ruby started helping her with her bag. "You are safe; you may come across some kiwis, rodents, and birds, but nothing dangerous." She held the boat as Maia stepped off onto shore. "There will be a clearing just up a bit where you might find it has been used before." She caught Maia's deep exhale. "Hey, hun, you will be fine. This is why you are here, to find yourself." Maia heard the boat creak as Ruby pushed themselves back into the water.

"Two nights. See you in a few days." Watching them go, Maia bent down, picking up her bag, water, and bucket. "Great." She turned around, looking at the dense bush, trying to calm her panic. She looked back at the water. She was all alone. Wikitoria stood there watching the boat disappear up the shoreline. Exhaling, she turned around, seeing the little path etched into the dirt. She reached down for her bag, water, and bucket. "Ok, Wiki." She sighed.

Let's get a fire going before it gets dark. They'd been back at camp about twenty minutes. When Maia had heard the bell ring through the bush mid-morning, she'd been lying in her handmade shelter deep in thought, writing about her plans for the next few years. Spending this time alone had really opened her eyes to what she wanted to do with herself. Hearing her name being called, Maia quickly chucked her notebook and things in her backpack, stamped out her embers, and said goodbye to her old self. "Oh my god!" Naydeen flopped down next to her on the rock.

They'd been picked up in the same boat. "I can't believe we just survived that! That was insane!" "Mmm." Maia nodded, her eye falling to the track, waiting for the others to arrive. She acknowledged the girl beside her who had just experienced what she had. "Did you write in your notebook?" "Heaps! Drew some pictures, too. You?" Naydeen asked. "You make any great revelations?" Just at that moment, they spotted movement on the track.

The others were back. Behind Jake and Millie, Wikitoria dragged herself up into the clearing. She looked like shit. "Oh my god, Wiki looks like she got lost or something." Maia noticed how skinny she looked, her toned arms looking soft, her whole presence deflated. "Wow, she had a rough couple of nights." Maia watched her throw her bag down, irritated.

Naydeen noticed the concerned look. She smiled to herself, getting up. "She'll be glad to have you to sleep next to tonight." Maia's brow knitted as she watched her leave her sitting there alone again. She turned to catch Wikitoria's eyes finding her. She saw her instant sigh of relief. "Hi." She gave her a little wave. Wikitoria smiled, giving her a little nod, her hand rising to wave but only reaching her stomach as she wandered off toward the kitchen.

The camp got quiet pretty quickly as they dropped off one by one, finding the comfort of their own beds. Coming back from a warm shower, Maia noticed Wikitoria sitting alone at the fire pit with her eyes closed. She thought about leaving her there, but... The scent of peaches hit her nose. Wikitoria came back from her peace, opening her eyes to the white towel-wrapped blonde sitting beside her. She blinked a few times not sure if she was real.

She exhaled, coming back to the present. "How long have you been there?" Maia squeezed out her still-damp hair. "A minute." She watched Wikitoria stretch her back, relaxing again. Her friend didn't seem herself. She sat forward. "Do you wanna talk about it?" Wikitoria was quiet for a moment before her eyes fell on her. "My flint fell out of my pocket when I jumped off the boat. I didn't know until it was too late." It took Maia a moment before she realized what she meant. Her eyes widened.

"You had no fire the whole time?!" "Nope." Wikitoria untucked her arms, reaching out to the warmth before her. "Aww, Wiki!" Maia moved closer, throwing her arms around her and rubbing her arms. "Are you ok?" She hugged her. Wikitoria welcomed it. "Yeah." She admitted. "Let's just say I'm no longer afraid of the dark." She laughed a little, a tear threatening to escape as her emotions surfaced. Maia could feel her. She didn't quite know what to say but continued rubbing her arms. "We're back now, warm water, warm beds." She reached up, touching her chin, turning her to look at her. "We're safe now. Come on." She stood up, reaching out for her hand. "You need some sleep." Maia stirred.

She felt a draft replace the warmth she had been curled up against. Her bunk creaked, and on opening her eyes, she caught Wikitoria climbing back onto the bunk across from her.

"You okay?" Wikitoria pulled her blankets up, curling herself into their warmth. "We have to get up soon." She sighed, looking at her. "Yeah, I am." "Okay." Maia reached her hand out. Wikitoria moved over, reaching out and taking her hand in her own. "Thanks for caring." "Mmm." Maia dropped her hand, feeling sleep taking hold. Wikitoria tucked her arms back up under her blanket.

She hadn't been able to sleep even though her body was tired enough. Looking down at Maia, fast asleep in her bunk, she had quietly jumped down and slipped in beside her. Within moments, she was asleep. Not thinking she could get back to sleep now, she lay there watching the darkness becoming lighter. Those couple of nights in the bush had been really tough. Her eyes had been open; she could hear every sound of the rodents around her searching out her snacks. She'd ended up using that to her advantage.

She put her bag a few feet away from her spot, thinking at least they weren't sniffing at her feet. This meant she had starved herself. The first day, all her stomach did was growl and protest its hunger. By day two, she wasn't hungry anymore. Besides, she had no flint to light a fire. She had found it floating in the branches of the bush roots. Cold and alone, her internal fight was a battle of its own. The lights flicked on, and the moans started. She sat herself up without thought and started putting her shoes on. Maia sat up, swinging her legs over the side. The yawn stretched across her face. Opening her eyes, she watched Wikitoria quietly tying her shoes. "Morning." Wikitoria looked up. Giving her a little smile, she reached for her hat and got up.

Maia watched her go. She slipped her feet into her shoes, unable to get her friend out of her thoughts. She just didn't seem right. Hearing the siren, she quickly grabbed her hat and ran outside. After a few laps of the beach, Maia found herself in charge of breakfast for the morning. Wikitoria picked up the tongs, selecting a couple of bacon pieces; Maia stepped over, slapping a big spoon of cream mushrooms on her plate. Dropping a toast on her plate, Maia grinned, seeing the questioning look on her face. "Mai, I'm really not that hungry." Maia reached over, sliding an egg and a squirt of tomato sauce on there. "When was the last time I made you breakfast? Just eat it." Maia stopped momentarily, watching her turn and sit at one of the tables.

Wikitoria really did seem out of sorts since her solos. "Maia, the eggs!" "Yip!" She turned back to her tasks. Wikitoria quietly flicked through the pages in her notebook. She'd drawn some pictures in there over the last few days, but nothing special. She felt Ruby's eyes fall on her. This was pointless; she had nothing to say. "Maia, would you like to share with us today?" Maia looked up, seeing everyone looking at her. "Umm, ok." She pulled herself to her feet. Taking a calming breath, she flicked through her notebook. "Umm, well, the last few days and nights have been…I've done a lot of thinking and, I guess, soul-searching.

Not much more you can do isolated in the bush." They all laughed. She wet her lips. "I came here because I wasn't sure of my path. I wanted to be a psychologist. I was diverting off, but after spending so much time, I guess in my head, it still fascinates me." She relaxed. "So, I've decided to head down to Otago after this to get my master's." "Well…" They all clapped as she sat back down. Ruby praised her. "I'm glad this has opened up this path for you, and I wish you all the best." Wikitoria found her washing out her clothes. She dropped her stuff in the outdoor sink. "Well, you made that decision quickly." Maia turned around from hanging up her shirt. "That's why I came here." "Bullshit, you came here for me," Wikitoria said, turning the tap on fill boar and wetting them both. "Wiki!" Maia jumped, reaching over and turning her tap off.

"What has got into you? You haven't been the same since you came back from…" "What, my nights of hell!" She slammed her fists in the water. It went flying everywhere. Maia stepped back. She'd never seen her like this before. "You can't go to Otago! It's too far away." Wikitoria continued. "Why not?" "Because I need you!" She snapped. "You said so yourself!" "No, you need…" "You, I need you, Maia, that's all!" "No, you need to face whatever this is!" Maia snapped. "Why did YOU come here in the first place!" She stepped closer. "It was to forget about me; remember, you told me loud and clear! You were moving out!" "I can't!" "Well, you are going to have to!" Maia growled, seeing the tension in her eyes.

She threw her towel over the line, picking up her stuff. "Seriously, you have issues, Wiki." "I do not!" "You are holding on to shit. You need to deal with Wiki until you can face whatever it is and who you really are..." She indicated, knowing Wikitoria knew precisely what she was talking about. "there is no us." "Maia, get back here!" Wikitoria yelled as she walked off from her. Kicking the basin, water splashed over her shoes. "God damn it!" Stopping, she looked at her shaking hands; her heart was racing. She took a deep breath, trying to calm herself down. "Jesus Christ, Wiki." She said to herself. She was losing it. Something was really wrong.

Tia looked up, seeing the young woman approaching her. "Kiaora Wikitoria. Kei te pehea koe?" Wikitoria sat down beside her. "Ngaro." She sighed. "Totally lost." "Hmm." Tia stopped what she was doing. "May I?" She noticed Wikitoria's notebook in her back pocket. Wikitoria reached back, handing it over. "There is not much in there." She watched the quiet woman with the moko kauae study her drawings. "I haven't..." "You haven't got to the core of why you are here yet, child." Wikitoria sat back a moment.

She hadn't been called a child in years. "Tell me, my girl, you seem to seek approval to be yourself." She closed her notebook, handing it back. Wikitoria wet her lips a little, confronted by her directness. Tia put her hand on her arm. "I see you. Others see you, yet you do not see yourself." She gave her a little smile. "Your fight is only with yourself. Overcome that, and you will set yourself free." Watching her get up, Wikitoria sat there, taken aback by how real this woman who didn't know her was just then. "Hmm." She opened her notebook, analyzing her pictures. Everything became clear after seeing the heart she drew the day up the mountain. She did need Maia but needed to find her own courage first.

Chapter 7

Wikitoria looked up at the Rockwall as she looped the rope through her buckles. "Hi." Millie stopped beside her. Wikitoria flicked her eyebrows, determined to focus on what she was doing. "You know you tan up real nice." Millie moved closer, helping straighten out her line. "Makes your eyes even brighter."

She flicked her eyebrow, unashamed of her flirting. Wikitoria watched her a moment. Usually, this behaviour freaked her out, but today... She turned around, giving Millie her full attention. That killer smile of hers came to her cheeks. Millie blushed slightly, feeling her eyes trail over her. Wikitoria leaned in. "See you up there." She winked. Millie swallowed quickly, wetting her lips as she watched the taller girl stretch her arm up, getting a firm grip before moving up the wall. Naydeen walked past, seeing the look on her face. She laughed.

"You ok, Millz?" She looked up and saw Wikitoria climbing the wall. "Mmhmm." Millie bit her lip, crossing her arms. She sighed. "Just admiring the view." Naydeen flicked her eyes back up the wall. She wasn't into women, but she had to admit Wikitoria was mighty fine. "Hmm." She crossed her arms and was about to leave. "As long as you are only looking." Her eyebrow rose, walking off. She saw Maia working on a task with Jade. "I'd watch out for that one."

Maia looked up, following her nod toward Millie. Not saying anymore, Jade sat back, confused. "What did she mean, watch out for that one? Who are we watching?" Maia looked up, noticing Wikitoria confidently climbing up the wall. Sighing, her eyes trailed back to her teammate, quietly stepping closer to the wall, obviously enjoying the view above her. "Nothing." She turned back to her task.

It hadn't been something she'd wanted to do, but after conquering the Rockwall, Wikitoria approached Adam, seeing him checking on the ropes at the skywalk. Adam noticed her over his shoulder. He smiled to himself. "Think you're ready?" Wikitoria looked up at the ropes. Her heart started beating, but... she nodded. "Yip. Yeah, I think I wanna give it a try." "Okay." He picked up his helmet, handing her one. "Let's go." Clinton came jogging down to the water, seeing the others pulling up the kayaks. "Hey, anyone wanna do the skywalk? Wiki's up there."

Naydeen floated on up. "Did you say Wiki is?" "Yip. Jake, are you coming?" Maia saw Naydeen taking off her life jacket and pulling up her kayak. She floated up onto the sand. "Maia." She looked up. "Wiki's doing the skywalk!" She frowned. "There's no way she'd go up there." She climbed out onto the sand, pulling up the kayak. "She's scared of heights. She'd freeze!" "Well, apparently she is so... you coming?" Maia took her lifejacket off, watching the others head back up to camp. She suddenly felt her stomach drop thinking of Wikitoria up so high. "Oh god!" She picked up her shoes. She had to see this for herself.

WIkitoria's fingers tightened around the rail. Climbing up the ladder had been fine, but standing on the platform was different. "You can do it, Wiki!" She tried not to look down, but her eyes betrayed her. "Hey," Adam laughed gently, seeing her turn around with her eyes closed. "You can do this." He clipped her line in, throwing the extra down to Marco. "You set?!" He yelled down, watching him tighten up the tension. Marco gave him the thumbs-up. Maia entered the clearing, her eyes widening, seeing Wikitoria was really up there. Adam pulled her line around behind her, doing his final checks. "Trust me, nothing else will ever challenge you once you have done this." Wikitoria met his eyes. "Take a deep breath." He inhaled. She followed, exhaling as she turned around to face the thick rope between the trees.

"Take your time, focus. Concentrate on your footing and find your balance before you move on." He slapped his hand on her shoulder. "Trust me, we won't let you fall." He held onto the top rope for her. She stepped closer, exhaling again. "Stay focused." She put her hand up, tightening her fingers around the rope. Maia put her hand on her face, closing her eyes for a second. She took a deep breath as Wikitoria moved her foot onto the rope. Feeling the tension, Wikitoria slid her other foot in front, her hand gripping the rope on the left. Feeling the triangle wobble, she closed her eyes before concentrating on her balance. "Good, you got it," Adam said behind her. "Trust yourself."

Taking a breath, she opened her eyes, seeing the platform a few meters away. "Come on, Wik." She said to herself, bringing her back foot to the front. Maia's hand moved to her mouth nervously as Wikitoria wobbled a couple of times before she managed to lock in her knees. Taking another step, Wikitoria started to get the hang of it. Naydeen noticed the worry on Maia's face. "Hey," She nudged her. "Don't worry, she's got it." "Yeah." Maia relaxed a little, watching her take a couple more steps. Wikitoria stopped a moment. She was halfway. "You alright?" She heard Adam behind her. "Yip!" She yelled out. She took that moment to let her eyes fall on the small crowd watching her.

Jake, Clinton, Millie, Jazz, Naydeen, and a nervous Maia. "Hey, Maia!" She yelled down. "Didn't think I'd get up here, did you!" She swayed a little, playing around. Maia stepped closer. "Stop being cocky and get down from up there!" "You know I quite like this!" She went to step, and her shoe slipped. "Oh my god!" Maia freaked. "Woo." Wikitoria got back up, finding her balance. She looked down at the others, reacting slightly panicked. "Okay." She said to herself, deciding to finish this up. "Come on, Wiki, you crazy fucken gaybo." She heard herself say the words as she continued. "That's right…" She nodded to herself. "You're a gaybo Wiki. And you're in love with a white girl. That white girl down there." She was almost there.

"And if Aroha can be a happy gaybo," she stepped onto the platform. "Then so can you." She turned around, hearing the cheers go up. "chaarrhoo!" She yelled, raising her arms and giving the air a fist pump. "I did it, yeahaa!" She saw Adam clapping over on the other platform. "You gonna come back?" She took a moment, taking a breath. "Yeah." She nodded, seeing Maia below relieved. She put her hand back up on the rope. She could do this. She actually could do this!

There was no doubt that Wikitoria Tamati had made a breakthrough as she sat with the others of her team, the centre of attention strumming the guitar like she was the main act at the campfire that night. Following Jade out of the kitchen, Maia couldn't help but notice her mate on her high. Catching her eye, she nodded; she was proud of her. "Hey, wait…I've got one." Wikitoria indicated to Lindon on the other guitar.

"You know this one?" As the Mataara team joined them, Wikitoria broke out in song. Millie was quick to take her place next to her. Maia held back, sitting next to Frankie at the picnic table. Wikitoria was on a high. She'd never felt so alive in her life. It was no lie. She was singing this for Maia. Luckily, everyone knew it, so she wasn't singing it alone. Feeling her eyes on her, Maia decided she needed to leave. Wikitoria was basking in all her glory, and she just wanted an early night. Seeing her get up and make her way into the darkness, Wikitoria smiled to herself.

Finishing out the song, she handed the guitar to Naydeen. "Here, I'll be back." Seeing her heading into the darkness, Millie quietly followed her. Ruby tapped Tia on the arm, seeing the girl follow Wikitoria into the darkness. Tia sighed, shaking her head. She'd noticed the girl's interest in the striking, taller girl. She sipped her tea. "We'll talk about it tomorrow."

"Mai," Wikitoria whispered, her hand out, feeling for the big tree. She knew she was here somewhere. "Where are you? I really wanna tell you something." She heard the twigs break behind her. "Oh, there you are." She reached out, feeling the body walk into her hand. She relaxed, laughing a little, and welcomed her moving into her. Being pushed back against the tree, she felt her hands pulling her shirt up. "Okay." Wikitoria laughed. "A quicky in the bush, I gotcha." She felt the hand on her cheek and the lips seeking out hers. Maia was rougher than usual. "Babe,"

Wikitoria whispered, touching her hand that was seeking out hers, the hungry mouth biting into her neck. "Babe, slow down." Her hand was getting forced into their shorts, her fingers pushed into wet folds. She heard her moan, suddenly realizing this wasn't Maia! "What the hell?!" Yanking her hand out, she pushed the body away from hers. "No, don't stop." "Millie?!" Wikitoria moved away, shaking. "What the hell are you doing!?" Millie followed her. "You know you want this; it was just getting good." "Get the hell away from me!" Wikitoria ran up towards camp. She stopped beside the outside basins and turned on the tap, washing her hands. "Oh god!" She couldn't stop shaking. Her pulse was going crazy. Tears were threatening her eyes. Unable to catch her breath, she leaned over the sink, dry wrenching, her fingers feeling foreign on her hand.

Lying in her bunk, drawing in her notebook, Maia watched the others start rolling in. She couldn't help but notice the look on Millie's face. "Eek." She rolled over, knowing that was a 'lust after Wiki' look. Realizing she was clenching her teeth, she shook it off. What was there to be jealous of? "Night, guys." "Night." The lights flicked out, and Maia got comfortable. Hearing a creak beside her, she turned over, hearing Wikitoria next to her bunk. She realized just then that she didn't see her come in. "Hey." She whispered, reaching out.

She felt her jump away from her touch; the sound of the top bunk moving indicated she wasn't going to sleep across from her. Maia sighed. "Okay." She expected Wikitoria to be a bit more affectionate with her after today. She rolled over, disappointed. Wikitoria couldn't stop shaking. Her hand was sore from scrubbing. Her heart wanted to curl up in that bottom bunk with Maia, but she feared what had just happened. She couldn't close her eyes. She finally let her tears fall. Pulling her blanket over her head, she cried herself to sleep.

The body clock was now used to waking up early. Maia sat up, inhaling the new day. One more day, then they were off back to the mainland. She looked around to see who else was awake. The siren went off. "Ugh, is this almost over!" Jade sat up, throwing her legs over the side. "Tomorrow." Naydeen jumped down from her bunk, finding her shoes. Maia swung her legs over, reaching for her boots. The top bunk creaked. Looking up, she saw Wikitoria sit up, moaning. She jumped down just as Maia stood up, straightening herself out. Their eyes met. Maia's features suddenly hardened, and her hand came up. Wikitoria felt the impact on her cheek, knocking her off balance. Holding her cheek, she watched Maia storm out the door. Tears started coming to Wikitoria's eyes. Did Maia know?

There was no run today; they were straight into the obstacle course. Maia was steaming ahead. Trying to stay focused, her emotions were scrambled between anger, hurt, jealousy, and feeling just stupid that she cared so much. Wikitoria was lagging but managed to catch Naydeen on the wall. Waiting for the rope to swing back, Naydeen quickly looked at her teammate, puffing hard. Wikitoria saw her laugh.

"What?" She reached out for her rope. Naydeen grabbed hers, indicating the mark on her neck. "Don't let the bosses see that." "See what?" Wikitoria reached up, feeling her neck.

"No relationships, remember." "let's go, let's go!" Marco yelled up at her, seeing her stop. Swinging out, she hit the ground and started running. Then it dawned on her. Did Millie mark her? "Oh god." She quickly pulled up her singlet, removed it, and wrapped it around her neck. She picked up the pace; she had to catch up to Maia before it was too late.

Maia came around the corner, stepping up onto the piles. Millie and Frankie were just ahead of her. Picking up the pace, she met Millie up the rope wall. Millie felt the ropes swing below her; she missed her footing and slipped through. Maia reached up, giving her a push. "Hey! We're on the same team!" Maia stood on her hand, reaching up higher. "Today, we're not." Wikitoria came around the corner, hitting the piles. She could see Maia reaching the top of the rope wall, Millie stuck in the middle, holding her hand. "Damn it."

Wikitoria jumped off, racing for the ropes. Swinging it out, she climbed up, reaching past Millie. "Wiki, help me up!" "Get fucked!" She reached up, standing on her other hand. Climbing over the top, Maia was already crossing the bridge. "Maia, wait!" Maia stepped onto the platform; she looked back, seeing Wikitoria on the other side in her sports bra, her singlet around her neck. "what's this? Trying to hide your hickey!" "I swear I thought she was you!" Rolling her eyes, Maia made her way down. Wikitoria stepped onto the bridge.

Swaying, she made it to the other side. She floored it down the hill, giving chase. "Maia!" Speeding up, Maia started on the tyres. Wikitoria was close on her heels. Tapping through Wikitoria tried to reach out to her. "Mai, let me speak!" They ran, Maia just keeping ahead. "I don't want to know!" "Mai," Wiki reached out as they closed the line. "It's not what you think." She puffed, trying to turn her around. "Leave me alone!" Maia snapped, pushing her away. "Hey!" Wikitoria turned around, finding Ruby at her side. "This is inappropriate attire; get that shirt back on!" Wikitoria wet her lips, her eyes flicked over Maia as she tried to catch her breath. "Miss..." "Now!" Ruby pointed. Wikitoria let out a few breaths before she reached up, unwrapping her neck. Ruby's eyes widened. Pulling her singlet down, Wikitoria met her disapproval. "You need to come with me."

The door closed as Adam sat at the table with the others. Wikitoria sat in the middle of the room, all eyes on her. Ruby leaned forward. "You want to explain this?" Wikitoria sighed. What was she supposed to say? She scratched her head, moving uncomfortably in her seat. "The rules clearly state, no relationships." "Someone just took advantage of me; it's not..." "Wait, someone forced themselves on you?"

"I didn't know she had followed me. I thought it was..." "She?" "Wait..." Tia scratched her forehead, confused. "She forced herself on you?" She tilted her head. "But you thought she was someone else?" "No. Yes..." She shook her head. "No, I went for a walk and..." She paused a moment. She couldn't tell the truth that she hoped to meet with Maia again under the tree. She sat back. "Look, I think someone just got the wrong idea and... I let them take advantage of me." She sighed. Tia sat forward. "You let them take advantage of you?" Wikitoria closed her eyes.

She could feel herself back at that tree, realizing she was touching someone who wasn't Maia. She broke a little. "I thought it was someone else." She heard them all sit back. Adam said quietly, "Wikitoria, this is a serious allegation and something we don't tolerate here. Male or female."

He looked at his colleagues. "Do you feel comfortable telling us who did this to you?" She closed her eyes, feeling her emotions close to the surface. Millie came to mind, but so did Maia. Maia couldn't find out what had happened this way. She had to tell her herself. "No." Wikitoria looked up. "Okay." Ruby sat forward, speaking on behalf of her team. "I think it is fair to say that by what you have told us, it is safer and more comfortable for us to remove you from camp. As we finish tomorrow anyway, we will organize to get you back to the mainland today." She got the nod from Marco. "Are you sure you don't want to take this further, hun? You are in your rights; you're not alone?" "No." Wikitoria sat up, wiping the dampness out of her eye. "I just wanna go."

She walked into the room she'd shared with the other women for the last few weeks. She made her way down the back to get her stuff. She couldn't believe she was leaving like this, but at least she had achieved what she had come here for. Tucking her clothes in her bag, she turned around, seeing the bunk Maia had been sleeping in just by her. They were all at breakfast. "Wiki." She heard Tia at the door. "Yip." Taking out her notebook, she flicked to the page where she had drawn the heart. Ripping it out, she tucked it under Maia's pillow. "I hope we get to sort this out at home. See ya soon." She slapped her cap on her head and headed out the door.

"Nah, no way I've got you beat at that man." "In your dreams." Maia followed the other girls into their room. They were heading down for the last of the kayak races. Pausing a moment, she noticed Wikitoria's stuff was gone. "She's gone." "Who?" Jazz stepped closer with her gears. She suddenly noticed the empty corner. "Where's Wiki? Hey, Wiki's gone!" "What?" "Where is she?" "She left?" Maia looked up, seeing them all crowded around her and Wiki's space. "I don't know." She shrugged. "I haven't seen her since the obstacle." Hearing the bell, Jade turned around. "Guys, we've got to get going." "Yeah." Maia looked up, seeing Naydeen still standing there.

Her arms crossed. "Shoulda kept your lips to yourself." "That wasn't me." "What?" Naydeen stepped closer. "But you two..." She sat down opposite her. "Nah, she was all into you. She wouldn't..." "Yeah, well, she did, and now she got herself kicked out." Naydeen sat there a moment as Maia walked out. This didn't make sense. Wikitoria didn't show any interest in anyone except for Maia.

Standing up, her eye caught the paper sticking out from Maia's pillow. Seeing everyone was gone, she pulled it out. "This was worth it." She recognized the handwriting in the corner of the drawing. A heart on what looked like an edge with the sun coming up. "Wiki, I knew it." She sighed, putting it back. Shaking her head, she looked around the room, confused about what happened. Then her eye fell on the bed that was Millie's. Her eyebrows knitted. Picking up her stuff, she headed on out.

The breeze against her face was cooling it down. Wikitoria had her shades on, hiding from Marco the tears sitting there. As the boat bounced over the water, she held the brown paper bag with her pounamu, rings, and phone in. Catching a tear on her cheek, she looked back, seeing the others preparing for the kayak races.

"Is that Wiki?" Maia looked up, catching the boat heading out across the water. "What happened? Is she in trouble or something?" "Hey, now we're uneven; someone has to go twice." Jazz handed her a lifejacket. "You alright?" Maia caught Wikitoria's little wave. "Yip." She turned back to the activity. "I'm going to kick all your asses!" "Think you're the fastest?" Frankie was already in the water. "I am, and you're the first to go." Maia pushed in her kayak. "Eww, challenge is on!"

Chapter 8

"Yeah, just this one, thanks." Wikitoria indicated the two-story house. She got out, grabbing her bag from the boot. "Thanks, mate." She tapped the car, stepping up onto the curb. Finding her keys, she headed on up to the door. "Hola!" She yelled out, seeing if anyone was home. "Anyone in?" She chucked her keys down, making her way to the laundry; she might as well wash her stuff properly now, get it out of the way.

"Yo, is anyone home?" She made her way upstairs, checking the rooms. "Damn, guess I'm it. Yes!" She entered her room, flopping down on her bed. "Ahh, man, I missed you." She smelt her pillow, the soft fluffiness and laundry powder scent heaven to her nose. Then she caught a whiff of herself. "Oh man, I need a shower." Getting up, she headed to her drawers. She grabbed some clean underwear and looked in her wardrobe for some clean clothes. "Oh, what!" She flicked through her empty racks. "Maia!"

She'd cleaned her out. "Well." She turned around, grabbing her stuff. "let's see what you got. Fairs fair." She headed across the hall into Maia's room. "Since you've got my clothes, you owe me." She found a top and some jeans in her wardrobe. "that's just gonna have to do." Jade sat down on the sand next to Maia. "Sure, feels weird, Wiki not being here." Maia sighed. Why was everyone talking to her about Wikitoria? She continued drawing in the sand with her stick. "I wonder what happened?" Maia wet her lip.

She wanted to say she got caught making out with someone, but the thought just made her mad. "Don't know. Maybe she just had to go early." "True." Naydeen flopped down beside them, throwing her paddle down. "Can't believe I just bet Clinton again!" "It's that long stride of yours." "Jade, you're up!" Watching her go, Naydeen turned to Maia, quietly drawing in the sand. "She left you something; it's under your pillow." Maia looked up. "I wasn't snooping. It was just there." She sighed. "Pity you won't see her again." "Hmm." A little smile crossed her face. "I wish." She saw Naydeen tilt her head. She leaned closer. "Wiki's my flatmate.

In fact, these are her clothes. I stole them from her wardrobe 'cause I had nothing appropriate to wear." "What?!" Naydeen couldn't help but start to laugh. "Are you serious?" "Yip." Maia began to laugh with her. "So don't feel too bad for us. I'll still get to tell her she's an idiot." "An idiot is right." Naydeen relaxed. "So does that mean you two do have something going on?" Maia looked at her. "We did, but..." She subtly indicated to her neck. Naydeen sighed. "Then what was that about if it wasn't you?" "I know." Her eye fell on Millie out on the water.

"But she wasn't into her, even I could tell that." Naydeen looked at her. "I don't even think she knew it was there." Maia sighed, drawing in the sand. "She did try to tell me something about it; she thought it was me?" Their eyes met. "Maybe she really did think it was you, but..." Their eyes fell on Millie. "You think she made a move last night?" "She was pretty clingy, and we both know she was following her around like a bad smell." "Hmm." Maia threw her stick away, about to get up. "If she made a move on her, I'm gonna smack her."

"No, wait!" Naydeen stood up with her. "Wait, we have one more night. Let's just mess with her." Maia turned around, brushing the sand off her clothes. "Okay." She picked up a paddle. "What did you have in mind?" Tying up her freshly washed hair, Wikitoria stood back, checking herself out in Maia's clothes, her pounamu sitting nicely against the material. "This isn't too bad. Maybe I need to raid your wardrobe more often." Sighing, she leaned forward, seeing the fading mark on her neck. "What an idiot, Wik." Still, she could do nothing until Maia returned the following day. "So..." She looked at herself, feeling pretty confident in this get-up. "Might as well get this over with." She headed out to the lounge, picked up her keys and phone, and made her way out to her car.

She was off to see her whanau. Maia was sitting in her kayak, waiting for the race to begin. Naydeen was a few kayaks over. The top two from both teams, Frankie and Millie, joined them. Naydeen waved over at her. "Want me to take her out?" "No. Frankie." She gave her the thumbs up. Hearing the whistle, they took off. Frankie had some power in his stroke, but Naydeen was catching up to him. Millie was holding on, but Maia was coming up quickly behind her. Making the turn, Millie dug her paddle in just as Maia came steaming for her. "Maia, watch out!" Causing waves, Maia passed her, putting the power in to catch Frankie.

Naydeen was hot on his heels. Coming up beside him, she tapped his paddle. "Hey." His grip loosened. "You almost..." Maia came past the other side, tapping his tail. "Woo!" He lost his balance and tipped out. Popping out of the water, Millie strolled past, taking third place. Winning the team heat, Maia and Millie had to race one more time. Maia pulled down her cap, tightening up her ponytail. She had been waiting for this. "Go, Mai!" She heard Naydeen on the shoreline. "You got this!" Maia looked over her shoulder at Millie.

She had a slight smirk on her face. "Hey." Maia leaned over, catching her eye. "This is paybacks." "For what?" "Getting Wiki kicked out." The whistle went. Maia dug in, pulling herself away from the start line. Millie set off following her along the course. She was quickly catching up. Maia was speeding up. She hit the turn, digging her paddle in, the tail of the kayak cutting into the water. Turning sharply, her nose was pointed at Millie. Millie had to quickly aim for the left as

Maia straightened up, heading back to the finish line. She dug in, leaving Millie in the dust. Crossing the finish line, the cheers went up. Wikitoria would have been proud. Wikitoria's Ma came back with her cup of coffee.

"Weren't you scared?" They were talking about her experience at Outward. "The first night alone I was. I didn't get much of a chance to look around. It got dark pretty quick, and I had no fire, so." Her ma put her hand on hers. "You're crazy!" That caused a smile on her face. Wikitoria laughed. "Yeah, I know." "Well…" Her mama sat back. "I hope you got something out of all of this." "I did." Wikitoria nodded, tapping her cup. "I'm a lot more confident about being in the dark. I've conquered my fear of heights." "Oh, good!" Her mama sipped her tea. "And there's something else I've been meaning to deal with. Well, not deal with but come to terms with." "oh…" Her mama put down her cup, concern in her eyes.

Wikitoria took a deep breath. "You see, mama, what happened with Aroha and Aunty really traumatized me, so it has been hard for me to be truthful about it." She saw her mama's features change. She wet her lip a moment, trying to find the right words. "Aroha had to leave, and I hope you will not make me do the same." She searched her mama's eyes. Was she going to have to say it? The corner of her mama's lip curled for a second. She looked at her hands around her cup.

"Your aunt is a prude." Her Ma reached her hand over, taking her daughter's hand in her own. "I know you, Wikitoria." She shrugged her shoulders. "I see you." She laughed, squeezing her hand. "And trust me, I would be more shocked if you turned up here with one of those silly boys." They laughed. Wikitoria relaxed a bit. Her mama sat back, watching her baby. "So, does this girl have a name?" Wikitoria blushed a little. This was a new kind of conversation between them. "Maia." "Maia," Her mama nodded. "A strong Maori name." Wikitoria laughed. "She's white." "Ohh." Her Mama took a moment to adjust to these modern times. Wikitoria smiled, taking her mama's hand. "Don't worry, mama, you'll like her; you really will."

"Hmm." Her mama relaxed, squeezing her daughter's hand. She smiled. "If she's made you this happy, you better tell me more about her." Maia chucked her gear down on the floor next to her bunk. That last kayak race had really taken it out on her shoulders. Sitting down, she admitted she could really do with one of Wikitoria's massages right about now. Sighing, her eyes scrimped over the empty bunks. Remembering what Naydeen had said, she looked beside her, sliding her hand under her pillow. She felt the paper. It was from her notebook. -This was worth it- She read the writing in the corner.

Holding it out, it took her a moment to figure out what it was. It was rough, but it was the view of the mountains from the overnight camp. The sun coming up, and the heart was them. Her features softened, remembering how special that had been between them. "Oh, Wik." She sighed. Putting it back under her pillow, she sat there a moment. She thought about her trying to talk to her at the obstacle and then seeing her on the boat.

She could have easily dobbed Millie or herself in, but she hadn't. She'd given them both the chance to finish this experience. She thought about the milestones she'd made being here. Even Wikitoria. Millie crossed her mind. Had she achieved what she came here for? She sat back a moment. This psychologist started to be intrigued. She picked up her hat. Maybe she needed to find out. She found her washing out the last of her clothes. "Hi." "Hi," Millie looked up momentarily, not thinking anything of it until she noticed Maia had no washing.

She stopped and put her hand on her hip. Maia leaned on the basin. "Wiki could have got you kicked out, but she didn't." Maia started seeing her turn to continue her washing. "So, I take it she took the fall for you so you could finish this." Millie stopped. "I have no idea what the hell you are on about." Maia stood up. "The hickey on Wiki's neck." Millie stopped. "It was you, wasn't it?" "Look…" Millie glared up at her. "I don't know what this has to do with you. Unless…" She smirked to herself. "I sense a wee bit of jealousy?" Maia paused.

The brilliant comeback was there, but she was trying to be mature about this. She crossed her arms. "Did you even consider that maybe your actions got her kicked out? The rules are the rules." She saw her bite her lip. Sitting down,

Maia looked up at her. "If you don't mind me asking, Millz, how did you end up coming here? What's your why?" Millie turned around, hanging up her shirt. She looked back at her teammate. She sighed. "I needed to get out of home for a few weeks." She admitted.

"Thought it might..." she tried to find the words with her hands. "it might toughen me up a bit." She shrugged. "My stepdad is a bit of an arse." "Oh." Maia nodded. Now, it was starting to make sense. "And Wiki?" The girl smiled, taking a seat next to her. "Like a goddess." She blushed slightly, feeling kind of embarrassed. "I got this..." she waved her hand. "Real like butterflies in my stomach when she was around me. It was addictive." She laughed a little. She shrugged. "Made me weird." Maia relaxed. "You got weird, alright." She wet her lip, unsure if she should ask this. "Did you give her that hickey?" She watched her purse her lips. There was a hint of satisfaction but also a hint of guilt in her expression. "I got carried away." She scratched the back of her neck.

"It just happened." Maia just sat there, hoping she would open up more. Millie saw her patience. She shrugged. "We were having a good night, and everyone was on such a high." She wet her lips. "She took off, and I just thought she was going back to the rooms, but she headed towards the big tree and..." Maia looked away a moment, realizing Wikitoria had been looking for her. "She turned around, and I don't know, I think she was expecting someone else, but..." She moved uncomfortably. "It got pretty..." She let out a lustful sigh. "Then she realized it was me and took off. Man, I'm such an idiot." She put her head in her hands. "How could I think someone like her would be into a skinny nobody like me." She looked up at Maia. "She wasn't even gay."

Maia exhaled. She had to apologise to Wikitoria when she got home. She looked at the small girl beside her. "Does anybody know you're gay?" Millie sat up, wiping her eyes. "I think I'm bisexual. I still like guys, you know, but..." Maia nodded, smiling at her. "Has this experience helped you find out what kinda strong person you can be?" Millie sat up. It took her a moment, but she nodded. "Yeah, it has." She smiled. She turned to Maia, who was stretching her neck. "Thanks." Maia looked down at her. "For what?" Millie shrugged. "For caring. I don't get that much." "Hey." Maia stood up, indicating for her to stand. She reached out and pulled her into a hug. Millie hesitated a moment, then relaxed, welcoming the embrace. "You're an amazing young person, Millie.

I hope whatever you decide to do when you leave here makes you the happiest person in the world." "Thanks, Maia." "You're welcome." She threw her arm over her shoulder. "Come on, let's go eat." "There she is!" Wikitoria looked up at her ma before turning around and seeing her aunty walk in the front door. "Help me with these groceries, bub!" Getting up, Wikitoria gave her aunty a quick kiss on the cheek, taking the bags from her arms. "fuu, it was busy in there today! I almost turned around and headed straight back out!" She laughed, putting her handbag down on the table with her keys. "Come here; let me take a look at you." Putting the milk in the fridge, Wikitoria stepped closer, letting her mother's sister pull her into a hug.

"Look at this, stunning as always, my girl." She squeezed her. "She's just returned from one of those outdoor adventure things, sis." "oh…" Her aunty tilted her head. "I can see that pale skin of yours has blackened up. You always had a nice tone, like your father." "Hmm." Wikitoria nodded. She glimpsed over at her mama; this was her aunty, not shy to say what she was thinking. "Put the jug on, bub; make your aunty a cuppa." "It's getting late, hun. Are you going to stay?" Wikitoria put the last couple of dishes on the rack, wiping the bench. She sighed. "If that's okay, Ma." "Sure, babe." "Just move your cousin's stuff, bub.

Who knows when she'll be back for it." Her aunty said from the lounge. Her aunty watched her come past the table. "You sure there isn't a handsome Tane waiting at home for you, my girl? Gotta be a few in the city there with you." Wikitoria saw her mama roll her eyes. "you're okay, babe, beds made up." Wikitoria stopped. She looked at her aunty a moment. She knew she had to do this for her cousin, too. "Actually, Aunty, I do have a partner, but she isn't back till tomorrow." She saw her Aunty nod and then suddenly realized what she said.

Her eyes fell on her niece standing there quite comfortably. Her sister sitting at the table. "Gees, sis, what do they teach these kids at school these days?" She shook her head. She was just about to say something when Wikitoria came to sit beside her. "I love you, my Aunty." She met her eyes. "Both you and Ma have taught me and Aroha the most important life lesson. Unconditional love." She reached over, putting her hand on hers. She smiled a little. "At least you don't have to worry about us bringing those silly patu boys home.

Their smelly toe jams and stink breath." Her aunt looked at her a moment. Her hand came up. Wikitoria flinched, expecting a smack, but her aunty held her cheek. "My daughter doesn't even talk to me anymore. Don't you be like that to your mama, or I'll…" She tapped her cheek, giving her a playful smack. Wikitoria smiled. "She misses you too, Aunty." Wikitoria stood up, kissing her Aunty on the head. Seeing her Ma, she blew out a breath. "Night, ma." "Night, babe."

Epilogue

Maia couldn't believe this was over. "Seeya, mate!" "See ya!" She waved as Jade got in the van. "Are you going back by Bus?" "Yip." Naydeen dropped her bag, turning around to hug her. "You tell that boofhead to look me up sometime, okay?" She pulled back. "You guys are always welcome." "Thanks." She watched Naydeen get in the van and close the door. Maia picked up her bag and headed over to the waiting bus. "Just this one." "Yip." She handed the bus driver her bag.

Taking one last look around, she stepped up into the bus. "Time to go home." "Make sure you bring that girl of yours home to meet me." Wikitoria hugged her Mama. "I will, Mama." She looked next to her at her Aunty. Smiling, she hugged her. "When I catch up with my cousin, I'll tell her to be in touch." She felt her aunty squeeze her tighter. "Okay." She pulled her keys out of her pocket and opened her car door. "I'll see you." She started up the car, heading back to the city. "Thank you." Maia waved to the taxi driver.

Looking up at the two-story house, she dug around in her bag for her key. "I'm home!" She chucked her bag down, relieved to be back. It was quiet. "Anyone here?" She heard the key in the door. Wikitoria hadn't expected to see her standing there. "Hi." "Hi." She closed the door. "I didn't think you'd be back yet." "I only just got here." "I can see that." Wikitoria pointed to the camp clothes she was still in. She sighed. "Look, Mai…" "Wiki, it is okay." "No…" Wikitoria stepped closer. "Nothing happened.

Seriously, I followed you to the tree, and I thought…" "It's okay," Maia stepped closer, raising her hand. "I know." She sighed. "Millie explained what happened." "She did?" "Yeah." Maia rubbed her temple. "She was just confused and got a bit carried away with all the butterflies she was getting around you." Wikitoria laughed at her animation. "Her butterflies?" "Well…" Maia smiled, stepping closer. "Apparently, she thought you were like some kinda goddess." "Goddess?" "Aha." She touched her top. "She was definitely under your spell." That killer smile of Wikis crossed her cheeks. "She wasn't the only one." "Alright." Maia pushed her away, smiling. "Where have you been anyway? Isn't that mine?" Wikitoria followed her to the laundry. "I went home to see my Ma." Maia looked over her shoulder as she put her clothes in the washing machine.

Wikitoria leaned on the door frame. "I told her the truth." Maia turned around. "That I am in love with a girl named Maia." Maia pursed her lips. She wasn't expecting that. She turned around, continuing her task. "What did she say?" Wikitoria laughed to herself. "She said Maia, that's a strong Maori name. I said she's white, ma. Oh, she said." Maia turned the machine on and turned around. "She said, well, if she's made you this happy, I will have to meet her." Wikitoria watched her lean back against the machine.

She stepped into the room, taking her hands in her own. "I'm in love with you, Maia. And after these last few weeks with you, I know I want to be with you." Maia searched her eyes. "But Wiki, I'm not staying. You know I'm going." The corner of Wikitoria's lips curled. "I know." She nodded. She let go of her hand, touching her cheek. "That is why I need to know…" She searched her eyes. "Do you?" Her eyes fell to her lips. "Feel anything remotely the same as I do?" "oh…" Maia played along, pulling her by the shirt closer. "You want me to tell you that I love you?" Wikitoria smiled, moving into her. "Yeah, I do. Cause I'm pretty sure you do." She laughed as Maia pulled her into a kiss.

"Mmmm." Maia smiled into her lips. "Maybe." "Woo." They heard from the door. Maia looked over Wikitoria's shoulder at Tammy standing there. "Sorry, I didn't know use…" She looked them over, confused. Wikitoria was cleanly dressed in Maia's clothes, and Maia was a mess in Wikitoria's. "Where? Why are you?" "Long story, Tamz." "Yeah. We'll explain later." Maia looked up at Wikitoria, still against her. "But right now, I really need to get out of these clothes." She met her eyes, biting her lip. "You wanna join me?" Wikitoria grinned. "Sure." Leading her by the hand, they walked past a still-confused Tammy.

Heading to the bathroom, Wikitoria closed the door behind them. "Mai." She turned her around. "I am serious about us." Maia sighed. She took her hands in her own. "Wiki. I love you. Come with me."

 "To Otago?" "It's only for a few years. We can get a place of our own." Wikitoria's features relaxed. "Yeah?" "Yeah." Maia wrapped herself around her. "I wanna be with you, and if anything…" She pressed into her, getting a smile. "I've kinda got used to waking up with you." She pulled her top off, taking her bra with her. "And strangely showering with you." "Well…" Wikitoria pulled her shirt off, joining her in her quick clothing removal. "Maybe you needed to find me just as much as I needed to find you. Wikitoria me te Maia." Maia paused as she turned the shower on, stepping in. Wikitoria smiled as she stepped in with her.

 "Victory and confidence." She kissed her skin. "Gonna get that tattooed right here." Maia opened her eyes, letting the water fall down her hair. "Victory, is it?" "Aha." "Hmm." Maia took her hands, pushing her against the tiled wall. "I'll happily claim my victory." "ouu." Wikitoria winked with her killer smile meeting her lips. "I like the sound of that."

www.ingramcontent.com/pod-product-compliance
Lightning Source LLC
Chambersburg PA
CBHW070446170726
48291CB00005B/1615